A DIRGE FOR PRINCES

(A THRONE FOR SISTERS -- BOOK 4)

MORGAN RICE

ISBN: 978-1-64029-269-7

Books by Morgan Rice

THE WAY OF STEEL
ONLY THE WORTHY (Book #1)

A THRONE FOR SISTERS
A THRONE FOR SISTERS (Book #1)
A COURT FOR THIEVES (Book #2)
A SONG FOR ORPHANS (Book #3)
A DIRGE FOR PRINCES (Book #4)
A JEWEL FOR ROYALS (BOOK #5)

OF CROWNS AND GLORY
SLAVE, WARRIOR, QUEEN (Book #1)
ROGUE, PRISONER, PRINCESS (Book #2)
KNIGHT, HEIR, PRINCE (Book #3)
REBEL, PAWN, KING (Book #4)
SOLDIER, BROTHER, SORCERER (Book #5)
HERO, TRAITOR, DAUGHTER (Book #6)
RULER, RIVAL, EXILE (Book #7)
VICTOR, VANQUISHED, SON (Book #8)

KINGS AND SORCERERS
RISE OF THE DRAGONS (Book #1)
RISE OF THE VALIANT (Book #2)
THE WEIGHT OF HONOR (Book #3)
A FORGE OF VALOR (Book #4)
A REALM OF SHADOWS (Book #5)
NIGHT OF THE BOLD (Book #6)

THE SORCERER'S RING
A QUEST OF HEROES (Book #1)
A MARCH OF KINGS (Book #2)
A FATE OF DRAGONS (Book #3)
A CRY OF HONOR (Book #4)
A VOW OF GLORY (Book #5)
A CHARGE OF VALOR (Book #6)
A RITE OF SWORDS (Book #7)
A GRANT OF ARMS (Book #8)
A SKY OF SPELLS (Book #9)

CHAPTER ONE

Kate sprinted for the docks Finnael had told her about, moving faster than anyone else could have, praying that she would be in time. The vision of her sister lying gray and dead haunted her, pushing her forward with all the speed her powers could give her. Sophia couldn't be dead.

She couldn't.

Kate could see the royal soldiers down in the village, pulling together now around their leader. Another time, Kate might have stopped to fight them, simply for the harm that the Dowager had done in her life. Now, though, there was no time. She ran for the boats, trying to pick out the one Sophia had been on in her vision.

She saw it ahead, a dual-masted vessel with a seahorse for a prow. She ran for it, leaping as she got close to clear the railing and land lightly on the deck of the ship. She could see sailors staring at her, some of them reaching for weapons. If they had done anything to harm her sister, she would kill every last one of them.

"Where is my sister?" she demanded, the words ringing out.

Perhaps they recognized the resemblance, even though Kate was shorter and more muscled than Sophia, and her hair was hacked boyishly short. They pointed mutely toward the cabin at the rear of the ship.

As she stormed toward it, Kate saw a large, balding, bearded man struggling back to his feet.

"What happened here?" she demanded. "Quickly, I think my sister is in danger."

"Your sister is Sophia?" the man said. He still looked confused by whatever had knocked him down. "There was a man... he hit me. Your sister is in the cabin."

Kate didn't hesitate. She walked to the cabin and kicked the door hard enough to splinter it open. Inside...

She saw a forest cat in one corner, large and gray-furred, growling softly. She saw Sebastian there, kneeling there with a dagger in his hands, wet with blood almost to the wrists. He was howling with tears, but that meant nothing. A man could cry with remorse, or with guilt, just as easily as anything else.

On the floor beside him, Kate could see Sophia, lying corpse still, her flesh as gray as anything Kate had seen in her vision. There

1

was blood pooling on the floor beside her, and a wound in her chest that could only have come from one weapon.

"She's dead, Kate," Sebastian said, looking over at her. "She's dead."

"*You're* dead," Kate bellowed. She'd told Sebastian once that she couldn't forgive the way he'd hurt Sophia. This, though, was beyond anything he'd done before. He'd tried to murder her sister. Anger flooded through Kate then, and she surged forward.

She hit Sebastian, knocking him away from her sister. He rolled up, the knife still in his hand.

"Kate, I don't want to hurt you."

"Like you hurt my sister?"

Kate kicked him in the stomach and then grabbed his arm, wrenching it until the knife clattered to the floor. He managed to pull clear before she could break the limb, but Kate wasn't done with him yet.

"Kate, I didn't do this, I—"

"*Liar!*" She ran forward, grabbing him and bundling him back through the doorway as much through speed as through the enhanced strength the fountain had given her. She burst out into the sunlight with him, then managed to get a grip on Sebastian's legs, lifting him. She flung him over the side of the ship to plunge down toward the docks. He landed on them headfirst, sprawling bonelessly in unconsciousness.

Kate wanted to jump down after him. Wanted to kill him. There was no time though. She had to get back to Sophia.

"If he wakes up," Kate said to the captain, "kill him."

"I'd do it now," the big man said, "but I have to get this ship moving."

Kate saw him point to where the royal soldiers were descending on the ship, moving toward it with grim determination.

"Do what you can," Kate said. "I have to help my sister."

She ran back into the cabin. Sophia was still too still, too bloodied. Kate couldn't see her chest rising or falling. Only the faintest flicker of thoughts within her told Kate that there was any life there at all. Kate knelt by her, trying to gather herself, trying to remember what Finnael the sorcerer had taught her. He'd brought a plant back to lush green life, but Sophia wasn't a plant, she was Kate's sister.

Kate reached for the space within her where she could see the energy around things, where she could see the soft golden glow that had faded almost to nothing around Sophia. She could feel that energy now, and Kate could remember what it had felt like to pull energy out of the plant, but pulling energy away wasn't what she needed to do.

She reached out, seeking other sources of energy, seeking the power that she needed to do this. She sank into it, trying to find any energy that she could. Kate could feel it then; feel it beyond the confines of this room, beyond the narrow bounds that defined her own flesh.

She felt it then, the instant of connection so huge, so overwhelming, that Kate didn't think she could hold onto it. It was too much, but if it meant saving Sophia, Kate had to find a way to do it. She grabbed for the power around her…

…and found herself feeling the whole of the kingdom, every life, every hint of power. Kate could feel the plants and the animals, the people and the things that represented older, stranger powers. Kate could feel it, and she knew what the energy was: it was life, it was magic.

She took power as delicately as she could, in fragments from a hundred places. Kate felt a patch of grass brown in the Ridings, a few leaves fall from trees on the slopes of Monthys. She only took the barest amount from each place, not wanting to do more harm than that.

Even so, it felt like trying to contain a flood. Kate screamed with the effort of trying to contain it all, but she held. She had to.

Kate poured it into Sophia, trying to regulate it all, trying to force it to do what she wanted. With the plant it had simply been a case of adding energy, but would that work here? Kate hoped so, because she wasn't sure that she knew enough about healing wounds to do anything else. She gave Sophia the energy that she'd borrowed from the world, bolstering the thin gold line of her life, trying to build it into something more.

Slowly, so slowly that it was almost imperceptible, Kate saw the wound start to close. She kept going, until the flesh there was perfect, but there was still more to do. It wasn't enough to have a perfect-looking corpse. She kept pushing energy into her sister, hoping against hope that it would be enough.

Finally she saw Sophia's chest start to rise and fall once more. Her sister was breathing on her own, and for the first time, Kate had the sense that she wasn't going to die. Relief flooded through her at that thought. Sophia didn't wake, though, her eyes staying closed no matter how much energy Kate used. Kate wasn't sure that she could hold onto the power any longer. She let it go, falling back to the deck in exhaustion as if she'd just run a dozen leagues.

That was when she heard the shouts of fighting from beyond the cabin. Kate forced herself to her feet, and it wasn't easy. Even if the energy to restore Sophia hadn't come from her, channeling it had still taken an effort. Kate managed to stand, drawing her blade and making it to the door.

Beyond, soldiers in royal uniforms were forcing their way onto the ship, while sailors struggled to push them back. She saw the captain charge forward, cutting a man down using a long knife, while another sailor pushed a man back from the railing with a billhook. She also saw a sailor killed by the thrust of a soldier's sword, another fall backward as a pistol sounded.

Kate all but staggered forward, managing to lunge with a thrust that took a soldier through the armpit, but barely managing to parry a blow from the butt of a musket. She stumbled and the man stood over her, reversing the weapon to bring a bayonet to bear.

Then Kate heard a roar, and the forest cat leapt past her, slamming into the man, its teeth ripping into his throat. The beast snarled and leapt at another, and now the soldiers hesitated, pulling back.

Kate had to kneel there and watch it, because she was too exhausted to do more than that. When she saw one of the soldiers aiming a pistol at the cat, she drew a dagger and threw it overhand. The weapon went off and he fell back from the boat.

Kate saw the cat leap over the side, onto the docks, and a second later she heard a scream as it struck again.

"Get this boat out to sea!" she yelled. "We're dead if we stay here!"

The sailors leapt to do it, and Kate forced herself up again, trying to plug the gap. Some fought, and they were like defenders at a parapet, pushing back the clambering foes. The forest cat snapped and snarled, leaping at those who forced their way aboard, swiping with claws and clamping down with needle-sharp teeth. Kate didn't know when her sister had acquired a companion like that, but it was certainly loyal—and deadly.

If she had been at full strength, she might have taken on the soldiers by herself, moving among them, running and killing. As it was, she could barely muster the energy to thrust down at them alongside the sailors. Those pushed past Kate, as if trying to shield her from the fighting. Kate just wanted them to focus on getting the ship away from the docks.

Slowly, the ship did start to move. The sailors used oars and long poles to push it clear, and Kate felt the shift of the deck under their efforts. A solider leapt at the ship and fell short, falling between the boat and the docks.

Below, Kate saw the forest cat still snarling and killing, hemmed in by soldiers. Kate suspected that her sister wouldn't want her companion abandoned, and in any case, the forest cat had saved them. She couldn't just leave it.

"You need to get aboard," she yelled, then realized the stupidity of expecting it to understand that. Instead, she summoned up the little power she had left, wrapping the need to get aboard with an image of the boat leaving, and threw it at the creature.

It turned its head, sniffed the air once, and bounded for the boat. Kate saw its muscles bunch, and then it leapt. Its claws dug into the wood of the ship as it pulled itself up the side, and then it settled on the railing pushing its head against Kate's hand and purring.

Kate stumbled back, feeling the solidity of a mast at her back. She all but slid down it to the deck, sitting there because she no longer had the strength to stand. But that didn't matter anymore. They were already well away from the docks, only a few scattered shots marking the presence of their attackers there.

They'd done it. They were safe, and Sophia was alive.

At least for now.

CHAPTER TWO

Sebastian woke to pain. Total, complete pain. It seemed to surround him, throbbing through him, absorbing every fraction of his being. He could feel the pulsing agony in his skull where he'd struck it as he fell, but there was another repetitive pain, bruising his ribs as someone tried to kick him awake.

He looked up and saw Rupert looking down at him from possibly the only angle where his brother didn't look like some golden ideal of a prince. His expression certainly didn't match that ideal, looking as though, had it been anyone else, he would have cheerfully cut their throat. Sebastian groaned in pain, feeling like his ribs might have broken under the impact.

"Wake up, you useless idiot!" Rupert snapped. Sebastian could hear the anger there, and the frustration.

"I'm awake," Sebastian said. Even he could hear that the words were anything but clear. More pain flooded through him, along with a kind of foggy confusion that felt as though he'd been hit over the head with a hammer. No, not with a hammer; with the whole world. "What happened?"

"You got thrown from a boat by a girl, that's what happened," Rupert said.

Sebastian felt the roughness of his brother's grip as he hauled him back to his feet. When Rupert let go, Sebastian staggered and almost fell again, but managed to catch himself in time. None of the soldiers around him moved to help, but then, they were Rupert's men, and probably had little love for Sebastian after his escape from them.

"Now it's your turn to tell *me* what happened," Rupert said. "I went through this village from end to end, and they finally told me that was the boat your *beloved* was taking." He made it sound like a curse word. "Since you were thrown off it by a girl with the same look to her—"

"Her sister, Kate," Sebastian said, remembering the speed with which Kate had propelled him from the cabin, the anger there as she had thrown him. She'd wanted to kill him. She'd thought that he'd...

He remembered then, and the image of it was enough to make him stop, standing there in blank unresponsiveness, even as Rupert

6

decided it would be a good idea to slap him. The pain of that felt like just one more iota added to a mountain of it. Even the bruises from where Kate had thrown him felt like nothing compared to the raw pit of grief that threatened to open up and claim him at any moment.

"I said, what happened to the girl who fooled you into being her fiancé?" Rupert demanded. "Was she there? Did she escape with the rest of them?"

"She's dead!" Sebastian snapped without thinking. "Is that what you want to hear, Rupert? Sophia is dead!"

It was as if he were looking down at her again, seeing her pale and lifeless on the cabin floor, blood pooled around her, the wound in her chest filled by a dagger so slender and sharp that it might as well have been a needle. He could remember how still Sophia had been, no hint of movement to mark her breathing, no brush of air against his ear when he'd checked.

He'd even pulled the dagger out, in the stupid, instinctual hope that it would make things better, even though he knew that wounds were not so easily undone. All it had done was widen the pool of blood, cover his hands in it, and convince Kate that he'd murdered her sister. It was a miracle, put like that, that she'd only thrown him from the boat, not cut him to pieces.

"At least you did one thing right in killing her," Rupert said. "It might even help Mother to forgive you for running off like this. You have to remember that you're just the spare brother, Sebastian. The dutiful one. You can't afford to upset Mother like that."

Sebastian felt disgust in that moment. Disgust that his brother would think he could ever hurt Sophia. Disgust that he saw the world like that at all. Disgust, frankly, that he was even related to someone who could see the world as just his plaything, where everyone else was on some lower level, there to fit into whatever roles he assigned.

"I didn't kill Sophia," Sebastian said. "How could you think I could *ever* do something like that?"

Rupert looked at him in obvious surprise, before his expression shifted to one of disappointment.

"And there I was thinking that you'd finally grown a backbone," he said. "That you'd decided to actually be the dutiful prince you pretend to be and get rid of the whore. I should have known that you would still be completely useless."

Sebastian lunged at his brother then. He smashed into Rupert, sending the pair of them tumbling to the wooden slats of the docks.

Sebastian came up on top, grabbing at his brother, swinging a punch down.

"Don't you talk about Sophia like that! Isn't it enough for you that she's gone?"

Rupert bucked and twisted underneath him, coming up on top for a moment and throwing a punch of his own. The tumbling momentum of the fight kept going, and Sebastian felt the edge of the dock against his back a moment before he and Rupert plunged into the water.

It closed over them as they fought, their hands locked on one another's throats almost through instinct. Sebastian didn't care. He had nothing left to live for, not when Sophia was gone. Maybe if he ended up as cold and dead as her, there was a chance that they might be reunited in whatever lay beyond death's mask. He could feel Rupert kicking at him, but Sebastian barely even acknowledged the tiny extra hint of pain.

He felt hands grabbing at him then, hauling him out of the water. He should have known that Rupert's men would intervene to save their prince. They pulled Sebastian and Rupert from the water by their arms and their clothes, hauling them up onto dry land and all but holding them up as the cold water seeped through them.

"Let go of me," Rupert demanded. "No, hold him."

Sebastian felt the hands tighten on his arms, holding him in place. His brother hit him then, hard in the stomach, so that Sebastian would have doubled up if the soldiers hadn't been holding him. He saw the moment when his brother drew a knife, this one curved and razor edged: a hunter's knife; a skinning knife.

He felt the sharpness of that edge as Rupert pressed it to his face.

"You think you get to attack me? I've ridden halfway across the kingdom because of you. I'm cold, I'm wet, and my clothes are ruined. Maybe your face should be too."

Sebastian felt a bead of blood form under the pressure of that edge. To his surprise, one of the soldiers stepped forward.

"Your highness," he said, the deference in his tone obvious. "I suspect that the Dowager would not wish us to allow *either* of her sons to be harmed."

Sebastian felt Rupert go dangerously still, and for a moment, he thought that he would do it anyway. Instead, he pulled the knife away, his anger sliding back behind the mask of civility that usually disguised it.

"Yes, you're right, soldier. I wouldn't want Mother angry that I had... miss-stepped."

It was such a benign term to use when he'd been talking about cutting Sebastian's face to pieces only moments before. The fact that he could switch like that confirmed almost everything Sebastian had heard about him. He'd always tried to ignore the stories, but it was as though he'd seen the real Rupert both here, and earlier, when he'd tortured the gardener at the abandoned house.

"I want all of Mother's anger reserved for you, little brother," Rupert said. He didn't hit Sebastian this time, just clapped a hand to his shoulder in a brotherly fashion that was undoubtedly an act. "Running off like this, fighting her soldiers. *Killing* one of them."

Almost too fast to follow, Rupert spun, stabbing the one who had raised an objection through the throat. The man fell, clutching the wound, his expression of shock almost matched by those around him.

"Let us be clear," Rupert said, in a dangerous voice. "I am the crown prince, and we are a long way from the Assembly of Nobles, with its rules and its attempts to contain its betters. Out here, I will *not* be questioned! Is that understood?"

If it had been anyone else, he would have quickly found himself cut down by the other soldiers. Instead, the men murmured a chorus of assent, each one seeming to know that anyone cutting down a prince of the blood would be the one responsible for reigniting the civil wars.

"Don't worry," Rupert said, wiping the knife. "I was kidding about cutting your face. I won't even say that you killed this man. He died in the fighting around the ship. Now, thank me."

"Thank you," Sebastian said in flat tones, but only because he suspected that it was the best way to avoid further violence.

"Besides, I think Mother will believe a tale of your uselessness more than one of your murderousness," Rupert said. "The son who ran away, couldn't get there in time, lost his lady love, and got himself beaten up by a girl."

Sebastian might have thrown himself forward again, but the soldiers were still holding him tight, as if expecting exactly that. Perhaps, in a way, they were even doing it for his own protection.

"Yes," Rupert said, "you make a far better tragic figure than one of hate. You look the very picture of grief right now."

Sebastian knew that his brother would never understand the truth of it. He would never understand the sheer pain eating through his heart, far worse than any of the aches from his bruises. He would never understand the grief of losing someone he loved, because Sebastian was sure now that Rupert didn't love anyone except himself.

9

Sebastian had loved Sophia, and it was only now that she was gone that he could begin to understand how much, simply by seeing how much of his world had been ripped away in the moments since he'd seen her so still and lifeless, beautiful even in death. He felt like some shambling thing from one of the old tales, empty except for the shell of flesh surrounding his grief.

The only reason he wasn't crying was because he felt too hollow to do even that. Well, that and because he didn't want to give his brother the satisfaction of seeing him in pain. Right then, he would even have welcomed it if Rupert had killed him, because at least that would have brought an end to the infinite expanse of pain seeming to stretch out around him.

"It's time for you to come home," Rupert said. "You can be there while I report everything that has happened to our mother. She sent me to bring you back, so that's what I'm going to do. I'll tie you over a horse if I have to."

"You don't have to," Sebastian said. "I'll go."

He said it quietly, but even so, it was enough to get a smile of triumph out of his brother. Rupert thought that he'd won. The truth was that Sebastian simply didn't care. It didn't matter anymore. He waited for one of the soldiers to bring him a horse, mounted up, and heeled it forward with leaden limbs.

He would go home to Ashton, and he would be whatever kind of prince his family wanted him to be. None of it would make a difference.

Nothing did, now that Sophia was dead.

CHAPTER THREE

Cora was more than grateful when the ground started to level out again. It seemed as though she and Emeline had been walking forever, although her friend didn't show any of the strain of it.

"How can you just keep walking like you aren't tired?" Cora asked, as Emeline continued to press forward. "Is it some kind of magic?"

Emeline looked back. "It's not magic, it's just... I spent most of my life on Ashton's streets. If you showed that you were weak, people found ways to prey on you."

Cora tried to imagine that, living somewhere where there was the chance of violence any time anyone showed weakness. She realized that she didn't have to imagine it, though.

"In the palace, it was Rupert and his cronies," she said, "or the noble girls who thought they could abuse you just because they were feeling angry at something else."

She saw Emeline cock her head to the side. "I would have thought that it would be better in the palace," she said. "At least you didn't have to dodge the gangs or the slave takers. You didn't have to spend your nights hunkered down in coal cellars so that no one would find you."

"Because I was already indentured," Cora pointed out. "I didn't even have a bed in the palace. They just assumed that I would find a corner to sleep in. That, or some noble would want me in their bed."

To Cora's surprise, Emeline put her arms around her in a hug. If there was one thing Cora had learned on the road, it was that Emeline wasn't usually a demonstrative person.

"I saw some nobles once, out in the city," Emeline said. "I thought that they would be something brighter and better than one of the gangs, until I got closer. Then I saw one of them beating a man senseless just because he could. They were exactly the same."

It seemed strange, bonding like this over how harsh their lives had been, but Cora did feel closer to Emeline than she had at the start of this. It wasn't just that they'd been through a lot of the same things in their lives. They'd traveled a long way together now too, and there was still the prospect of more miles to come.

"Stonehome will be there," Cora said, trying to convince herself as much as Emeline.

"It will," Emeline said. "Sophia saw it."

It felt strange, putting so much trust in Sophia's powers, but the truth was that Cora *did* trust her, absolutely. She would gladly trust her life to the things that Sophia had seen, and there was no one she would rather share the journey with than Emeline.

They kept going, and as they headed west, they started to see more rivers, in networks that connected like capillaries leading to bigger arteries. Soon, there seemed to be almost as much water as land, so that even the fields in between were semi-flooded things, people farming in mud that threatened to turn into marsh at any moment. Rain seemed to be a constant, and while occasionally Cora and Emeline huddled down out of the worse of it, for the most part they pressed on.

"Look," Emeline said, pointing to one of the riverbanks. All Cora could see at first were reeds rising beside it, disturbed here and there by the movement of small animals. Then she saw the coracle upturned on the bank like the shell of some armored creature.

"Oh no," Cora said, guessing what Emeline intended.

Emeline reached out to put a hand on her arm. "It's all right. I'm good with boats. Come on, you'll enjoy it."

She led the way to the coracle, and all Cora could do was follow, silently hoping that there would be no oars. There was a paddle, though, and it seemed to be all Emeline needed. Soon, she was in the coracle, and Cora had to jump in beside her or be left walking along the bank.

It was faster than walking, Cora had to admit. They skimmed down the river like a pebble thrown from some giant hand. It was as relaxing as it had been sitting on the cart. More relaxing, since they'd spent half the time on the cart jumping off to help push it up hills and out of mud. Emeline seemed to be enjoying piloting it too, navigating the changes in the river as it went from rough to smooth water and back again.

Cora saw the moment when the water shifted, and she saw Emeline's expression shift in the same instant.

"There's… something there," Emeline said. "Something powerful."

What have we here? a voice asked, sounding in Cora's mind. *Two fresh young things. Come closer, my darlings. Come closer.*

Ahead, Cora saw… well, she wasn't quite sure what she saw. At first, it seemed like a woman made from water, but a flicker of light later, it seemed like a horse. The urge to go toward it was overwhelming. It felt as though there was safety ahead.

No, it was more than that; it felt as if it was *home* waiting for her there. The home that she'd always wanted, with warmth, a family, safety...

That's it. Come to me. I can give you everything you want. You will never be alone again.

Cora wanted to urge the coracle forward. She wanted to dive from it, to be with the creature that promised so much. She half stood, ready to do just that.

"Wait!" Emeline called out. "It's a trick, Cora!"

Cora felt something settle around her mind, a wall rising up between her and the promises of safety. She could see Emeline straining, and knew that the other girl had to be the one doing it, blocking the power pushing at them with her own talents.

No, come to me, the thing urged, but it was a distant echo of what it had been.

Cora looked at it, really looked at it, now. She saw the swirling water there; saw the currents around it that would drown anyone foolish enough to pass through them. She remembered old stories of river spirits, kelpies, the kind of dangerous magic that had turned the world against all of it.

She saw the water start to shift beneath the coracle, and only realized what was happening as the current started to drag it forward.

"Emeline!" she yelled. "It's pulling us in!"

Emeline remained still, shaking with obvious effort as she fought to keep the creature from overwhelming them both. That meant that it was up to Cora. She grabbed for the coracle's paddle, aiming for the shore and paddling with all the strength she had.

At first, it seemed that nothing was happening. The current was too strong, the kelpie's pull too total. Cora recognized those thoughts for what they were and pushed them aside. She didn't have to paddle against the current, just to its side. She pulled at the water with it, forcing the coracle to move through sheer strength of will.

Slowly, it began to shift off course, moving closer to the bank as Cora paddled.

"Hurry," Emeline said beside her. "I don't know how much longer I can keep this up."

Cora kept going, and the coracle moved by what felt like inches, but it did move. It grew closer, and closer, until finally Cora thought that the reeds might be in reach. She grabbed for them, managing to get hold of a handful of them and using them to pull their tiny vessel close to the shore. She dragged the coracle to the riverbank, then leapt out, grabbing for Emeline's arm.

13

She pulled her friend up onto the riverbank, seeing the coracle pulled in by the current. Cora saw the kelpie rear up in apparent anger, smashing down on the small vessel and reducing it to splinters.

As soon as they were on dry land, Cora felt the pressure on her mind easing, while Emeline gave a gasp and rose to her feet under her own power. It seemed that, off the water, the kelpie couldn't touch them. It reared up again, then plunged down, disappearing out of sight.

"I think we're safe," Cora said.

She saw Emeline nod. "I think... maybe we'll stay off the water for a while, though."

She sounded exhausted, so Cora helped her away from the riverbank. It took a while to find a path, but once they did so, it seemed natural to follow it.

They kept going along the road, and now there were more people than there had been in the north. Cora saw fisher-folk coming in from the riverbanks, farmers with carts full of goods. She saw more people coming in from all around now, with loads of cloth or herds of animals. One man was even herding a flock of ducks that ran ahead of him as sheep might have for someone else.

"There must be a traveling market," Emeline said.

"We should go," Cora said. "They might put us back on the road for Stonehome."

"Or they might kill us as witches the moment that we ask," Emeline pointed out.

Even so, they went, making their way along the paths with the others until they saw the market ahead. It was on a small island amidst the rivers, the route fordable at any one of a dozen points. On that island, Cora saw stalls and auction spaces for everything from goods to livestock. She was just grateful that no one was trying to sell any of the indentured today.

She and Emeline made their way down to the island, wading across one of the fords to reach it. They kept their heads low, blending into the crowds as much as possible, especially when Cora saw the masked figure of a priestess wandering through the crowd, dispensing her goddess's blessings.

Cora found herself drawn to a space where players were performing *The Dance of St. Cuthbert*, although it wasn't the serious version that had sometimes been put on in the palace. This version featured a lot more bawdy humor and excuses for sword fights, the company obviously knowing its audience. When they were done, they took a bow, and people started to call out the names of plays and skits, hoping to see their favorite performed.

"I still don't see how we can find someone who knows the way to Stonehome," Emeline said. "At least, not without as good as declaring ourselves to the priests."

Cora had been thinking about that too. She had an idea.

"You will see if people start thinking about it, won't you?" she asked.

"Maybe," Emeline said.

"So we get them thinking about it," Cora said. She turned to the players. "What about *The Stone Keeper's Daughters*?" she called out, hoping that the crowd would block any sight of her.

To her surprise, it worked. Perhaps it was because it was a daring, even dangerous, play to call for: the story of how a stonemason's daughters proved to be witches and found a home far from those who would hunt them. It was the kind of play that could get someone arrested for performing it in the wrong place.

They performed it here, though, in all its glory, masked figures representing priests chasing after the young men playing the women's parts for fear of bad luck. All the while, Cora looked at Emeline expectantly.

"Well, is it getting them thinking about Stonehome?" she asked.

"Yes, but that doesn't mean... wait," Emeline said, turning her head. "See that man there, selling wool? He's thinking about a time he went there to trade. That woman... her sister went there."

"So you have a direction for it again?" Cora asked.

She saw Emeline nod. "I think we can find it."

It wasn't much of a hope, but it was something. Stonehome still lay ahead, and with it, the prospect of safety.

CHAPTER FOUR

From above, the invasion looked like the sweep of a wing enfolding the land it touched. The Master of Crows enjoyed that, and he was probably the only one in a position to appreciate it, his crows giving him a perfect view as his ships swept in to shore.

"Perhaps there are other watchers," he said to himself. "Perhaps the creatures of this island will see what is coming for them."

"What is that, sir?" a young officer asked. He was bright and blond-haired, his uniform shining with the effort of polishing.

"Nothing you need to be concerned with. Prepare to land."

The young man hurried off, with the kind of spring in his movements that seemed to long for action. Perhaps he thought himself invulnerable because he fought for the New Army.

"They're all food for the crows eventually," the Master of Crows said.

Not today, though, because he had picked his landing sites with care. There were parts of the continent beyond the Knifewater where people shot at crows almost as a matter of course, but here they had yet to learn the habit. His creatures had spread out, showing him the spots where defenders had set cannon and barricades in preparation for an invasion, where they had hidden men and fortified villages. They had created a network of defenses that should have swallowed an invading force whole, but the Master of Crows could see the holes in them.

"Begin," he commanded, and bugles blared, the sounds carrying across the waves. Landing boats lowered, and a tide of men swept into shore in them. Mostly, they did it in silence, because a player did not announce the placing of his pieces on a gaming board. They spread out, bringing in cannon and supplies, moving swiftly.

Now the violence began, in exactly the ways that he had planned, men creeping around the ambush sites of his enemies to descend on them from the rear, weapons pounding the hidden knots of foes who wanted to stop him. From this distance, it should have been impossible to hear the screams of the dying, or even the musket fire, but his crows relayed everything.

He saw a dozen fronts at once, the violence blooming into multifaceted chaos as it always did in the moments after a conflict had begun. He saw his men charging up a beach into a knot of peasants, swords swinging. He saw horses disembarking while around them, a company fought to maintain its beachhead against a militia armed with agricultural tools. He saw both points of slaughter and hard-fought bravery, although it was hard to tell the two apart.

Through his crows' eyes, he saw a group of cavalry gathering a little way inland, their breastplates shining in the sun. There were enough that they could potentially punch a hole in his carefully coordinated web of landing sites, and although the Master of Crows doubted they knew the correct spot to strike, he could not take that risk.

He extended his concentration, using his crows to find a suitable officer nearby. To his amusement, he found the young man who had been so eager before. He focused, the effort of making one of the beasts carry his words far greater than simply looking through their eyes.

"There are cavalry north of you," he said, hearing the croak of the crow's voice as it repeated the words. "Circle to the ridge to your west and take them as they come for you."

He didn't wait for a response, but instead sent the crow into flight, watching from above as the men obeyed his orders. This was what his talent gave him: the ability to see more, to spread his reach further than any normal man could have. Most commanders found themselves mired in the fog of war, or hamstrung by messengers who couldn't move fast enough. He could coordinate an army with the ease a child might have shown moving tin soldiers around a table.

Below his circling bird, he saw the cavalry come thundering in, looking every inch some elegant army out of legend. He heard the blare of the muskets that started to cut them down, then saw the waiting soldiers charge into them, quickly turning their storybook charge into a thing of blood and death, pain and sudden anguish. The Master of Crows saw man after man fall, including the young officer, caught through the throat by a stray blade.

"All food for the crows," he said. It didn't matter; that small battle was won.

He could see a more difficult battle around the dunes that led up toward a small village. One of his commanders hadn't been fast enough to follow his orders, which meant that the defenders had dug in, holding the route to their village even against the larger force. The Master of Crows stretched, then clambered down into a landing boat.

"To shore," he said, pointing.

The men with him set to their work with the speed that came from long practice. The Master of Crows watched the progress of the battle as he got closer, hearing the screams of the dying, seeing his forces overwhelm group after group of would-be defenders. It was obvious that the Dowager had ordered the defense of her kingdom, but clearly not well enough.

They reached the shore, and the Master of Crows strode through the battle as if he were taking a stroll. The men around him kept low, muskets raised as they looked for threats, but he walked tall. He knew where his enemies were.

All his enemies. He could already feel the power of this land, and sense the movement in it as some of the more dangerous things there reacted to his arrival. Let them feel him coming. Let them know fear at what was to come.

A small knot of enemy soldiers leapt up from a hiding place behind an upturned boat, and there was no more time to think, only act. He drew a long dueling blade and a pistol in one smooth motion, firing into the face of one of the defenders, then running another through. He swayed aside from an attack, struck back with lethal force, and kept moving.

The dunes were ahead, and the village lay beyond them. Now the Master of Crows could hear the violence without having to resort to his creatures. He could pick out the clash of blade on blade with his own ears, the boom of muskets and pistols echoing as he approached. He could see men struggling with one another, his crows letting him pick out the points where defenders knelt or lay, their weapons trained on anything that approached.

He stood there in the middle of it all, daring them to fire at him.

"You have one chance to live," he said. "I need this beach, and I am prepared to pay you for it with your lives and those of your families. Lay down your arms and leave. Better yet, join my army. Do these things, and you will survive. Continue to fight, and I will see your homes razed."

He stood there, waiting for an answer. He got it when a shot rang out, the pain and impact of it slamming through him so hard that he staggered, falling to one knee. Right then, though, there was too much death around to stop him so easily. The crows were being well fed today, and their power would heal anything that did not kill him outright. He pushed power into the wound, closing it as he stood.

"So be it," he said, and then charged forward.

Ordinarily, he did not do this. It was a foolish way of fighting; an old way that had nothing to do with well-organized armies or efficient tactics. He moved with all the speed that his power gave him, dodging and running as he closed the distance.

He killed the first man without stopping, plunging his sword deep and then wrenching it clear. He kicked the next to the ground, then finished him with a sweeping stroke of his blade. He snatched up the man's musket with one hand and fired it, using the sight of his crows to tell him where to aim.

He plunged forward into a cluster of men hiding behind a barricade of sand. Against the slow advance of his forces, it might have been enough to delay them, creating time for more men to come to bear. Against his wild charge, it made no difference. The Master of Crows leapt the sand walls, jumping into the midst of his enemies and cutting in every direction.

His men would be following behind, even if he had no concentration to spare to look through the eyes of his crows for them. He was too busy parrying sword strokes and axe blows, striking back with vicious efficiency.

Now his men were there, pouring over the sand barricades like the incoming tide. They died as they did it, but now it didn't matter to them, so long as they were there with their leader. It was what the Master of Crows had been counting on. They showed surprising loyalty for men who were little more than crow food to him.

With their numbers behind him, it wasn't long before the defenders were dead, and the Master of Crows let his men push forward toward the village.

"Go," he said. "Slaughter them for their defiance."

He watched the rest of the landings for a few minutes more, but there didn't seem to be any other major choke points. He had chosen his spot well.

By the time the Master of Crows reached the village, parts of it were already aflame. His men were moving through the streets, cutting down any of the villagers they found. Most were, anyway. The Master of Crows saw one dragging a young woman from the village, her fear matched only by the soldier's obvious enjoyment of it.

"What are you doing?" he asked as he got closer.

The man stared at him in shock. "I... I saw this one, my lord, and I thought—"

"You thought you'd keep her," the Master of Crows finished for him.

"Well, she'd fetch a fine price in the right place." The soldier dared a smile that seemed designed to make the two of them part of some grand conspiracy.

"I see," he said. "I did not order that though. Did I?"

"My lord—" the soldier began, but the Master of Crows was already raising a pistol. He fired it so close that the other man's features all but disappeared in the blast of it. The young woman beside him seemed too shocked even to scream as her attacker fell.

"It is important that my men learn to act in accordance with my orders," the Master of Crows said to the woman. "There are places where I allow captives, and others where it is agreed that none but the gifted are to be harmed. It is important that discipline is maintained."

The woman looked hopeful then, as if thinking that this was all some mistake, in spite of the depredations of the others in the village. She looked that way right up to the point when the Master of Crows thrust his sword through her heart, the thrust sure and clean, probably even painless.

"In this case, I gave your men a choice, and they made it," he said as she clutched at the weapon. He pulled it out, and she fell. "It is a choice I intend to give much of the rest of this kingdom. Perhaps they will choose more wisely."

He looked around as the slaughter continued, feeling neither pleasure nor displeasure, just a kind of even satisfaction at a task accomplished. A step, at least, because after all, this was no more than the taking of a village.

There would be much more to come.

CHAPTER FIVE

Dowager Queen Mary of the House of Flamberg sat in the great chambers of the Assembly of Nobles, trying not to look too bored on her throne at the heart of things while the supposed representatives of her people talked, and talked.

Ordinarily, it wouldn't have mattered. The Dowager had long ago mastered the art of looking impassive and regal while the great factions there argued. Typically, she let the populists and the traditionalists wear themselves out before she spoke. Today, though, that was taking longer than usual, which meant that the ever-present tightness in her lungs was growing. If she did not finish with this soon, these fools might see the secret that she worked so hard to disguise.

But there was no hurrying it. War had come, which meant that everyone wanted their chance to speak. Worse, more than a few of them wanted answers that she didn't have.

"I merely wish to ask my honorable friends whether the fact that enemies have landed on our shore is indicative of a wider government policy of neglecting our nation's military capabilities," Lord Hawes of Briarmarsh asked.

"The honorable lord is well aware of the reasons that this Assembly has been wary of the notion of a centralized army," Lord Branston of Upper Vereford replied.

They continued to babble on, refighting old political battles while more literal ones were growing closer.

"If I might state the situation, so that this Assembly does not accuse me of neglecting my duty," General Sir Guise Burborough said. "The forces of the New Army have landed on our southeastern shores, bypassing many of the defenses that we put in place to prevent the possibility. They have advanced at a rapid rate, overwhelming those defenders who have tried to stop them and burning villages in their wake. Already, there are *numerous* refugees who seem to think that *we* should provide them with lodging."

It was amusing, the Dowager thought, that the man could make people running for their lives sound like unwanted relatives determined to stay too long.

"What of preparations around Ashton?" Graham, Marquis of the Shale, demanded. "I take it that they are heading this way? Can we seal the walls?"

That was the response of a man who knew nothing about cannon, the Dowager thought. She might have laughed out loud if she'd had the breath for it. As it was, it was all she could do to maintain her impassive expression.

"They are," the general replied. "Before the month is out, we might have to prepare for a siege, and earthworks are already being constructed against the possibility."

"Are we considering evacuating the people in the army's path?" Lord Neresford asked. "Should we advise the people of Ashton to flee north to avoid the fighting? Should our queen, at least, consider retreating to her estates?"

It was funny; the Dowager had never taken him for one interested in her well-being. He had always been quick to vote against any proposal she put forward.

She decided that it was time to speak, while she still could. She stood, and the room fell silent. Even though the nobles had fought for their Assembly, they still listened to her within it.

"To order an evacuation would start a panic," she said. "There would be looting in the streets, and strong men who might defend their homes otherwise will flee. I will stand here too. This is my home, and I will not be seen to run from it in the face of a rabble of foes."

"Far from a rabble, Your Majesty," Lord Neresford pointed out, as if the Dowager's advisors hadn't told her the precise extent of the invading force. Perhaps he just assumed that, as a woman, she wouldn't have enough knowledge of war to understand it. "Although I am sure that all the Assembly is eager to hear your plans to defeat it."

The Dowager stared him down, although that was hard to do when her lungs felt as though she might burst into a coughing fit at any moment.

"As the honorable lords know," she said, "I have deliberately eschewed too close a role in the kingdom's armies. I wouldn't want to make you all uncomfortable by claiming to command you now."

"I'm sure we can forgive it this once," the lord said, as if he had the power to forgive or condemn her. "What is your solution, Your Majesty?"

The Dowager shrugged. "I thought that we would start with a wedding."

She stood there, waiting for the furor to die down, the various factions within the Assembly shouting at one another. The royalists were cheering their support, the anti-monarchists griping about the waste of money. The military members were assuming that she was ignoring them, while those from the further reaches of the kingdom wanted to know what any of it meant for their people. The Dowager didn't say anything until she was sure that she had their attention.

"Listen to yourselves, babbling like frightened children," she said. "Did your tutors and your governesses not teach you the history of our nation? How many times have foreign foes sought to claim our lands, jealous of their beauty and their wealth? Shall I list them for you? Shall I tell you about the failures of the Havvers Warfleet, the Invasion of the Seven Princes? Even in our civil wars, the foes that came from without were always pushed back. It has been a thousand years since anyone has conquered this land, and yet you panic now because a few foes have evaded our first line of defenses."

She looked around the room, shaming them like children.

"I cannot give our people much. I cannot command without your support, and rightly so." She didn't want them arguing about her power here and now. "I can give them hope, though, which is why today, in this Assembly, I wish to announce an event that offers hope for the future. I wish to announce the impending marriage of my son Sebastian to Lady d'Angelica, Marchioness of Sowerd. Will any of you seek to force a vote on the matter?"

They didn't, although she suspected that it was as much because they were stunned by the announcement as anything. The Dowager didn't care. She set off from the chamber, deciding that her own preparations were more important than whatever business it would conclude in her absence.

There was still so much to do. She needed to make sure that the Danses' daughters had been contained, she needed to make wedding preparations—

The coughing fit took her suddenly, even though she had been expecting it through most of her speech. When her handkerchief came away stained with blood, the Dowager knew that she'd pushed too hard today. That, and things were progressing faster than she would have liked.

She *would* finish things here. She would secure the kingdom for her sons, against all the threats, inside and out. She would see her line continue. She would see the dangers eliminated.

Before all of that, though, there was someone she needed to see.

"Sebastian, I'm so sorry," Angelica said, and then stopped herself with a frown. That wasn't right. Too eager, too bright. She needed to try again. "Sebastian, I'm so sorry."

Better, but still not quite right. She kept practicing as she made her way along the corridors of the palace, knowing that when the time came to actually say it in earnest, it would have to be perfect. She needed to make Sebastian understand that she felt his pain, because that kind of sympathy was the first step when it came to owning his heart.

It would have been easier if she'd felt anything but joy at the thought of Sophia being gone. Just the memory of the knife sliding into her brought a smile that she wouldn't be able to show in front of Sebastian when he got back.

That wouldn't be long. Angelica had beaten him home by riding hard, but she had no doubt that Rupert, Sebastian, and all the rest would return soon. She needed to be ready once they did, because there was no point in removing Sophia if she couldn't take advantage of the gap that left.

For now, though, Sebastian wasn't the member of their family she needed to worry about. She stood outside the Dowager's quarters, taking a breath while the guards watched her. When they swung the doors back in silence, Angelica set her brightest smile on her features and ventured forward.

"Remember that you've done what she wants," Angelica told herself.

The Dowager was waiting for her, seated on a comfortable chair and drinking some kind of herbal tea. Angelica remembered her deep curtsey this time, and it seemed that Sebastian's mother wasn't in a mood to play games.

"Please rise, Angelica," she said in a tone that was surprisingly mild.

Still, it made sense that she would be pleased. Angelica had done everything that was required.

"Sit there," the older woman said, gesturing to a spot beside her. It was better than having to kneel before her, although being commanded like that was still a small piece of grit rubbing against Angelica's soul. "Now, tell me about your journey to Monthys."

"It's done," Angelica said. "Sophia is dead."

"Are you sure of that?" the Dowager asked. "You checked her body?"

24

Angelica frowned at the questioning note there. Was nothing good enough for this old woman?

"I had to escape before that, but I stabbed her with a stiletto laced with the most vicious poison I had," she said. "No one could have survived."

"Well," the Dowager said, "I hope you're correct. My spies say that her sister showed up?"

Angelica felt her eyes widening slightly at that. She knew that Rupert wasn't back yet, so how could the Dowager have heard so much, so quickly? Maybe he'd sent a bird ahead.

"She did," she said. "She sailed off with her sister's corpse, on a boat heading for Ishjemme."

"Heading for Lars Skyddar, no doubt," the Dowager muttered. It was another small shock for Angelica. How could peasants like Sophia and her sister possibly know someone like Ishjemme's ruler?

"I've done what you wanted," Angelica said. Even to her, it sounded defensive.

"Are you expecting praise?" the Dowager asked. "Maybe a reward? Some petty title to add to your collection, maybe?"

Angelica didn't like being talked down to like that. She'd done everything the Dowager had required. Sophia was dead, and Sebastian would be home soon, ready to accept her.

"I have just announced your nuptials to the Assembly of Nobles," the Dowager said. "I would think that marrying my son would be reward enough."

"More than enough," Angelica said. "Will Sebastian accept this time, though?"

The Dowager reached out, and Angelica had to force herself not to flinch as the old woman patted her cheek.

"I'm sure I said that was part of *your* job. Distract him. Seduce him. Get down on your knees in front of him and beg, if you have to. My reports say that he's cloaked in grief as he comes home. Your job will be to make him forget all of that. Not mine, yours. Do a good job, Angelica." The Dowager shrugged. "Now get out. I have things to do. I have to make sure that you actually finished Sophia, for one thing."

The dismissal was abrupt enough to be rude. With anyone else, it would have been enough to warrant retribution. With the Dowager, there was nothing that Angelica could do, and that only made it worse.

Still, she would do what the old woman required. She would make Sebastian hers once he got home. She would be royalty by marriage soon, and that elevation would be more than reward enough.

In the meantime, the Dowager's uncertainty about Sophia gnawed at her. Angelica had killed her; she was sure of it, but...

But it wouldn't hurt to see what she could learn about events in Ishjemme, just to be certain. She had at least one friend there, after all.

CHAPTER SIX

Sophia could feel the rhythmic flow of the ship somewhere beneath her, but it was a distant thing, on the edge of her awareness. Unless she concentrated, it was hard to remember that she had ever been on a ship. She certainly couldn't find it, even though it was the last place that she could remember being.

Instead, she seemed to be in a shadowy place, filled with mist that shifted and billowed, fractured light filtering through it so that it seemed more like the ghost of a sun than its reality. In the mist, Sophia had no idea which way was forward, or which way she was supposed to go.

Then she heard the cry of a child, cutting through the fog more clearly than the sunlight. Somehow, some instinct told her that the child was hers, and that she needed to go to it. Without hesitating, Sophia set off through the mist, running toward it.

"I'm coming," she assured her child. "I'll find you."

It continued to cry, but now the mist twisted the sound, making it seem to come from every direction at once. Sophia picked a direction, plunging forward again, but it seemed that every direction she picked was the wrong one, and she got no closer.

The mist shimmered, and scenes seemed to form around her, set out as perfectly as performances on a stage. Sophia saw herself screaming in childbirth, her sister holding her hand as she brought a life into the world. She saw herself holding that child in her arms. She saw herself dead, with a physiker standing beside her.

"She wasn't strong enough, after the attack," he said to Kate.

That couldn't be right though. It couldn't be true if the other scenes were true. It could happen.

"Maybe none of it is true. Maybe it's just imagination. Or maybe they're possibilities, and nothing is decided."

Sophia recognized Angelica's voice instantly. She spun, seeing the other woman standing there, a bloody knife in her hand.

"You're not here," she said. "You can't be."

"But your child can?" she countered.

She stepped forward and stabbed Sophia then, the agony of it lancing through her like fire. Sophia screamed... and she was alone, standing in the mist.

She heard a child crying somewhere in the distance, setting off toward it because she knew instinctively that it was her child, her daughter. She ran, trying to catch up, even as she had the sense that she'd done this before…

She found scenes from a girl's life around her. A toddler playing, happy and safe, Kate laughing along with her because they'd both found a good hiding place under the stairs and Sophia couldn't find them. A toddler pulled from a castle just in time, Kate fighting against a dozen men, ignoring the spear in her side so that Sophia could run with her. The same child alone in an empty room, no parent there.

"What is this?" Sophia demanded.

"Only you would demand meaning from something like this," Angelica said, stepping from the mist again. "You can't just have a dream, it has to be filled with portents and signs."

She stepped forward, and Sophia raised a hand to try to stop her, but that just meant that the knife thrust into her under the armpit, rather than cleanly up through the chest.

She was standing in the mist, a child's cries sounding around her…

"No," Sophia said, shaking her head. "I won't keep going around and around this. It's not real."

"It's real enough for you to be here," Angelica said, her voice echoing from the mist. "What does it feel like, being a dead thing?"

"I'm not dead," Sophia insisted. "I can't be."

Angelica's laugh echoed the way her child's cries had before. "You can't be dead? Because you're that special, Sophia? Because the world needs you so much? Let me remind you."

She stepped from the mist, and now they weren't standing in mist, but in the cabin of the boat. Angelica stepped forward, the hatred on her face obvious as she thrust the blade into Sophia once more. Sophia gasped with it, then fell, collapsing into darkness as she heard Sienne attack Angelica.

She was back in the mist then, standing there while it shimmered around her.

"Is this death then?" she demanded, knowing that Angelica would be listening. "If so, what are you doing here?"

"Maybe I died too," Angelica said. She stepped back into view. "Maybe I hate you so much that I followed you. Or maybe I'm just everything you hate in the world."

"I don't hate you," Sophia insisted.

She heard Angelica laugh then. "Don't you? You don't hate that I got to grow up in safety while you were in the House of the

Unclaimed? That everyone accepts me at court while you had to run? That *I* could have married Sebastian without any problems, while you had to run away?"

She stepped forward again, but this time she didn't stab Sophia. She stepped past her, walking off into the mist. The mist seemed to reshape itself as Angelica passed, and Sophia knew that this couldn't be the real her now, because the real Angelica wouldn't have tired of murdering her quite so quickly.

Sophia followed in her wake, trying to make sense of it all.

"Let's show you a few more possibilities," Angelica said. "I think you'll like these."

Just the way Angelica said it told Sophia how little she would like it. Even so, she followed her into the mist, not knowing what else to do. Angelica quickly disappeared out of sight, but Sophia kept walking.

Now she was standing in the middle of a room where Sebastian sat, obviously trying to hold back the tears that fell from his eyes. Angelica was there with him, reaching out for him.

"You don't have to hold your emotions back," Angelica said in a tone of perfect sympathy. She put her arms around Sebastian, holding him. "It's all right to grieve for the dead, but just remember that the living are here for you."

She looked straight at Sophia while she held Sebastian, and Sophia could see the look of triumph there. Sophia started forward in anger, wanting to pull Angelica away from him, but her hand couldn't even touch them. It passed through without making contact, leaving her staring at them, no more than a ghost.

"No," Sophia said. "No, this isn't real."

They didn't react. She might as well not have been there. The image shifted, and now Sophia was standing in the middle of the kind of wedding that she could never have dared to imagine for herself. It was in a hall whose roof seemed to reach to the sky, nobles gathered in such numbers that they made even that seem small.

Sebastian was waiting by an altar along with a priestess of the Masked Goddess whose robes proclaimed her rank above the others of her order. The Dowager was there, seated on a throne of gold as she watched her son. The bride came forward, veiled and dressed in pure white. When the priestess threw back the veil to reveal Angelica's face, Sophia screamed...

She found herself in chambers she knew from memory, the layout of Sebastian's things unchanged from the nights she'd spent there with him, the fall of moonlight on the sheets straight from her memories of their time together. There were bodies tangled in those sheets, and in one another. Sophia could hear their laughter and their joy.

She saw moonlight fall on Sebastian's face, caught in an expression of pure need, and Angelica's, which held nothing but triumph.

Sophia turned and ran. She ran through the mist blindly, not wanting to see any more. She didn't want to stay in this place. She had to escape it, but she couldn't find a way out. Worse, it seemed that every direction she turned led back in the direction of more images, and even the images of her daughter hurt, because Sophia had no way of knowing which ones might be real and which were just there to hurt her.

She had to find a way out, but couldn't see well enough to find one. Sophia stood there, feeling the panic building in her. Somehow, she knew that Angelica would be following her again, stalking her through the mist, ready to thrust her blade home in her once more.

Then Sophia saw the light, glowing through the fog.

It built slowly, starting as a thing that barely pushed its way through the murk, then slowly becoming something bigger, something that burned the fog away the same way the morning sun might burn off morning dew. The light brought warmth with it, feeding life into limbs that had felt leaden before.

It flowed over Sophia, and she let the power of it pour into her, carrying with it images of fields and rivers, mountains and forests, a whole kingdom contained in that touch of light. Even the remembered pain of the wound in her side seemed to fade before that power. On instinct, Sophia put her hand to her side, feeling it come away wet with blood. She could see the wound there now, but it was closing, the flesh knitting together under the touch of the energy.

As the mist lifted, Sophia could see something in the distance. It took a few more seconds before enough burned away to reveal a spiral staircase leading up toward a patch of light, so far above that it seemed impossible to reach. Somehow, Sophia knew that the only way to leave this seemingly never-ending nightmare was to reach that light. She set off in the direction of the staircase.

"You think you get to leave?" Angelica demanded from behind Sophia. She spun, and barely managed to get her hands down in time as Angelica struck at her with the knife. Sophia pushed her back on instinct, then turned and ran for the stairs.

"You'll never leave here!" Angelica called out, and Sophia heard her footsteps following behind.

Sophia sped up. She didn't want to be stabbed again, and not just to avoid the pain of it. She didn't know what would happen if this place shifted again, or how long the opening above would last. She couldn't afford to take the risk either way, so she ran for the stairs, spinning as she reached them to kick out at Angelica and knock her back mid-thrust.

Sophia didn't stay to fight her, but instead sprinted up the stairs, taking them two at a time. She could hear Angelica following, but that didn't matter then. All that mattered was escaping. She continued up the stairs as they climbed, and climbed.

The stairs kept going, seeming to climb forever. Sophia continued to clamber up them, but she could feel herself starting to tire. She was no longer taking the steps two at a time now, and a glance over her shoulder showed her that the version of Angelica in whatever nightmare this was still followed her, stalking forward with a grim sense of inevitability.

Sophia's instinct was to keep climbing, but a deeper part of her was starting to think that was stupid. This wasn't the normal world; it didn't have the same rules, or the same logic. This was a place where thought and magic counted for more than the purely physical ability to keep going.

That thought was enough to make Sophia stop and delve deeper into herself, reaching for the thread of power that had seemed to connect her to an entire country. She turned to face the image of Angelica, understanding now.

"You aren't real," she said. "You aren't here."

She sent a whisper of power out, and the image of her would-be killer dissolved. She concentrated, and the spiral staircase disappeared, leaving Sophia standing on flat ground. The light wasn't high above now, but was instead just a step or two away, forming a doorway that seemed to open onto a ship's cabin. The same ship's cabin where Sophia had been stabbed.

Taking a deep breath, Sophia stepped through, and woke.

CHAPTER SEVEN

Kate sat on the deck of the ship as it scythed through the water, exhaustion preventing her from doing much more. Even with the time that had passed since she'd healed Sophia's wound, it felt as though she hadn't fully recovered from the effort.

From time to time, the sailors checked on her as they passed. The captain, Borkar, was especially attentive, running by with a frequency and deference that would have seemed amusing if he hadn't been so completely sincere about it.

"Are you all right, my lady?" he asked, for what seemed like the hundredth time. "Do you require anything?"

"I'm fine," Kate assured him. "And I'm not anyone's lady. I'm just Kate. Why do you keep calling me that?"

"It's not my place to say, my... Kate," the captain insisted.

It wasn't just him. All the sailors seemed to be walking around Kate with a level of deference that verged on the obsequious. She wasn't used to it. Her life had consisted of the brutality of the House of the Unclaimed, followed by the camaraderie of Lord Cranston's men. And there had been Will, of course...

She hoped that Will was safe. When she'd left, she hadn't been able to say goodbye, because Lord Cranston would never have let her go if she had. She would have given anything to be able to say it properly, or better yet, to bring Will with her. He would probably have laughed at the men who bowed to her, knowing how much that unwarranted politeness would annoy her.

Maybe it was something Sophia had done. After all, she'd played the part of a noble girl before. Maybe she would explain it all once she woke up. If she woke up. No, Kate couldn't think like that. She had to hope, even if it had been more than two days now since she'd closed the wound in Sophia's side.

Kate went through to the cabin. Sophia's forest cat raised its head as Kate entered, looking up protectively from where it lay across Sophia's feet like some furry blanket. To Kate's surprise, the cat had barely moved from Sophia's side in all the time the ship had been traveling. It let Kate ruffle its ears as she moved to her sister's bedside.

"We're both just hoping that she'll wake up, aren't we?" she said.

She sat beside her sister, watching her sleep. Sophia looked so peaceful now, no longer marred by the stiletto wound in her side, no longer gray with the pallor of death. She could have been asleep, except that she'd been asleep like this for so long that Kate was starting to worry she might die of thirst or hunger before she woke.

Then Kate saw the faint flicker of Sophia's eyelids, the barest movement of her hands against the bedclothes. She stared at her sister, daring to hope.

Sophia's eyes opened, staring straight at her, and Kate couldn't help herself. She threw herself forward, hugging her sister, holding her close.

"You're alive. Sophia, you're alive."

"I'm alive," Sophia reassured her, holding on as Kate helped her to sit up. Even the forest cat seemed happy about it, moving forward to lick both of their faces with a tongue like a blacksmith's rasp.

"Easy, Sienne," Sophia said. "I'm all right."

"Sienne?" Kate asked. "That's her name?"

She saw Sophia nod. "I found her on the road to Monthys. It's a long story."

Kate suspected that there were a lot of stories to be told. She moved back from Sophia, wanting to hear all of it, and Sophia all but fell back to the bed.

"Sophia!"

"It's all right," Sophia said. "*I'm* all right. At least, I think I am. I'm just tired. I could do with a drink too."

Kate passed her a water skin, watching Sophia drink deeply. She called out for the sailors, and to her surprise, Captain Borkar himself came running.

"What do you need, my lady?" he asked, then stared at Sophia. To Kate's shock, he fell to one knee. "Your highness, you're awake. We were all so worried about you. You must be starving. I'll fetch food at once!"

He hurried off, and Kate could feel the joy coming off him like smoke. She had at least one other concern, though.

"Your highness?" she said, staring over at Sophia. "The sailors have been treating me oddly ever since they realized I was your sister, but this? You're telling them that you're royalty?"

It sounded like a dangerous game to play, pretending to be royal. Was Sophia playing on her engagement to Sebastian, or pretending to be some foreign royal, or was it something else?

"It's nothing like that," Sophia said. "I'm not pretending anything." She took hold of Kate's arm. "Kate, I found out who our parents are!"

That was one thing that Sophia wouldn't joke about. Kate stared at her, barely able to believe the implications of it. She sat down on the edge of the bed, wanting to understand it all.

"Tell me," she said, unable to contain her shock. "You really think... you think that our parents were some kind of royalty?"

Sophia started to sit up. When she struggled with it, Kate helped her.

"Our parents were named Alfred and Christina Danse," Sophia said. "They lived, *we* lived, in an estate in Monthys. Our family used to be the kings and queens before the Dowager's family pushed them aside. The person who explained this said that they had a kind of... connection to the land. They didn't just rule it; they were part of it."

Kate froze as she heard that. She'd felt that connection. She'd felt the country spread out before her. She'd reached for the power in it. It had been how she'd been able to heal Sophia.

"And this is real?" she said. "This isn't some kind of story? I'm not going mad?"

"I wouldn't make this up," Sophia reassured her. "I wouldn't do that to you, Kate."

"You said that our parents *were* these people," Kate said. "Are they... did they die?"

She did her best to hide the pain that went through her with that thought. She could remember the fire. She could remember running. She couldn't remember what had happened to her parents.

"I don't know," Sophia said. "No one seems to know what happened to them after that. All of this... the plan was to head to our uncle, Lars Skyddar, and hope that he knows something."

"Lars Skyddar?" Kate had heard that name. Lord Cranston had talked about the lands of Ishjemme, and how they'd managed to keep out invaders using a combination of cunning tactics and the natural defenses of their icy fjords. "He's our uncle?"

It was too much to take in. Just like that, Kate had gone from having no family beyond her sister to having a family who had been kings and queens, who *did* rule in at least one far-off land. It was too much, too quickly.

On instinct, Kate found herself reaching for the locket that she wore around her neck. She took it out, looking down at the image of the woman within. She had a name for that woman now: Christina Danse. Her mother. That made her Kate Danse.

34

Kate smiled. She liked the sound of that. She liked the idea of having a family name that she knew, rather than just being Unclaimed, marked by the tattoo on her calf.

"What's that?" Sophia asked, and Kate realized that she wasn't looking at the locket, but at the ring she'd placed on the same chain for safekeeping. There was no doubt that Sophia recognized it. Of course she would, when it had been her engagement ring. "Where did you get that?"

There was no point in trying to hide it now.

"Sebastian gave it to me to give to you," she said. "But Sophia, you need to stay away from him."

"I love him," Sophia said, "and if he loves me—"

"He *stabbed* you," Kate insisted, feeling an echo of the anger that had been there when she'd first seen Sophia lying there near death. "He tried to murder you!"

Even given that, Sophia still shook her head. "That wasn't him."

"Because that's not how he really is?" Kate guessed. It sounded like the kind of excuse some farmer's wife might make when her husband got drunk and beat her. "Because he loves you really?"

"No," Sophia said. "I mean that it *wasn't him*. A noblewoman called Milady d'Angelica stabbed me, not Sebastian."

Kate hadn't met this noblewoman, but she hadn't been the one kneeling over Sophia's body.

"He was here," Kate insisted. "He had the knife in his hand. He was covered in your blood!"

"Maybe he was trying to save me," Sophia insisted.

"And maybe you're just reaching for anything you can find to defend him," Kate shot back. "Maybe you even really believe that this woman was here, rather than Sebastian, but I know what I saw."

"It was Angelica," Sophia insisted. "She stabbed me, and Sienne tore a piece out of her back as she ran. Please, Kate, I just want you to believe me. Sebastian wasn't the one who did this."

"He's done plenty of other things," Kate pointed out. "He was the one who sent you away so that you ended up in this mess in the first place. He said he wanted to find you, but as far as I can see all he did was lead half the royal army to hunt you. Even if he didn't stab you, he did nothing to try to save you."

"You can't blame him for not having the magic to heal me," Sophia said. She reached up for Kate, pulling her close. "I don't want to fight, Kate. You saved my life, and we're traveling together

35

now to find our family. I love Sebastian. Can't you just accept that?"

Kate wished she could, but as far as she could see, loving Sebastian had brought her sister nothing but pain. She took the ring from the chain around her neck, pressing it into Sophia's hand with bad grace.

"You should have this," she said. "If it were me, I'd take it and throw it into the ocean, or sell it for extra coin, but you'll probably take it as a promise."

Kate saw Sophia nod, and knew that her sister was thinking in those terms. She really thought that the prince whose hands had been covered in her blood would come to her and be the perfect husband. Kate saw her slip it onto her little finger, holding it there almost reverently.

"Why do you want him so much?" Kate demanded. "Why is it so important that things work out with him? You have a whole life ahead of you. You've just told me that we have a chance to find our family. You've told me that… goddess, I'm a princess, aren't I?"

"You're a princess," Sophia said with a faint smile, "and you will have to wear pretty ball gowns from now on."

"Not in a million years," Kate said. "And you're avoiding the point. You're not some Indentured girl anymore. You could have any man you wanted. So why him? And don't just tell me that you love him."

"Is love so stupid?" Sophia asked.

Kate found herself thinking about Will, but didn't say anything. If this was the way love made people think, then it *was* stupid.

"Kate, I need him," Sophia said.

"Why?"

"Because I'm pregnant with his child," Sophia said.

Kate stared at her. "You're pregnant?"

She hugged her sister again then.

"Of course, you realize what this means?" Sophia asked. "You're not just going to be a princess, Kate. You're going to be an *aunt*."

Kate hadn't thought of it like that, and just the thought of it was mildly terrifying. There were other, bigger, fears though. The two of them were heading off to a place Kate had never been to find a man they didn't know, all while her home was in the middle of an invasion.

She didn't know what their trip to Ishjemme would involve, but she suspected that it wouldn't be easy.

CHAPTER EIGHT

Sebastian shambled into the palace like a dead thing when he arrived, and not just because Rupert had made them ride hard on the way back south, apparently enjoying his discomfort.

The fact was that the world seemed too empty for anything else now that Sophia was gone.

"You should go get cleaned up," Rupert said with obvious amusement. "I'm sure Mother will want to speak to you as soon as she hears you're back."

He was clearly looking forward to the thought of what their mother would have to say, but he was still quick to leave Sebastian to it. Maybe he was that eager to get back to his carousing and his cronies. Maybe he was just certain that Sebastian didn't have any reason to go anywhere else now.

Every step back toward his rooms felt like Sebastian was dragging a lead weight attached around his heart. He'd barely slept since leaving the north, and not just because Rupert had taken a kind of cruel delight in pushing them to get back sooner. Every time he closed his eyes, Sebastian had seen Sophia lying there cold and dead on the floor.

He couldn't believe that she was gone. Sophia had only been in his life for the briefest of times, but it seemed impossible now that she had ever not been there. A world without her in it simply seemed wrong.

He went to his rooms, changing and cleaning himself up almost automatically. A servant brought food, but it might as well have been ashes for all that Sebastian tasted it.

"I heard that you were back."

He turned to see Angelica standing in the doorway. She was dressed in a gown of shimmering gray silk, stitched with silver.

"I'm sorry, Milady," Sebastian said, "but I'm really not in the mood for—"

She stepped forward, putting her arms around him without being asked.

"I'm glad you're safe," she said, holding him. "I know you won't believe it, but I am."

Sebastian could feel the presence of her there, warm and comforting and alive. He wanted to push away from her then, but couldn't bring himself to do it, not when she was the only person who seemed to be willing to offer the least crumb of kindness.

"I don't feel very safe," Sebastian said. "I feel…"

He couldn't keep the tears out of his eyes. He expected Angelica to run from that, to pull back for fear of staining the silk of her dress. Instead, she continued to hold onto him, forming the pillar that seemed to be holding up his world.

"What happened?" Angelica said.

Sebastian swallowed, not sure that he could bring himself to say it. "It's Sophia. She's… someone killed her."

"She's dead?" Angelica said, and Sebastian could see the shock of it on her face. "Oh, Sebastian, I'm so sorry."

"You didn't even like her," Sebastian pointed out.

He saw Angelica hesitate before she answered. "No, you're right. I was going to lie and say something kind, but I didn't like her. I thought that she was pretending to be someone she wasn't, and I didn't like that she was going to hurt you with it. But this… I know this must be hurting you even more. I don't want that, Sebastian."

Sebastian was surprised by how much even that helped. Just knowing that there was someone out there who cared about his grief was something.

"Do you know what happened?" Angelica asked. "Rupert went out after you, did he…?"

Sebastian shook his head. Just thinking about what had happened on the boat hurt. "I don't think so. Rupert was still searching when I found her. There was… there was blood everywhere."

The worst part of it was not knowing. Whoever had done this deserved to die, but instead, it felt as though they'd gotten away with their crime.

"I don't even know who did it," Sebastian said. "There has to be some reason for it, some *point* to it. I need to find out, Angelica. I need to find them."

She reached out, putting a hand on his arm. Her touch was as gentle as the silk of her dress. "Are you sure that's such a good idea, Sebastian? You're grieving, and maybe—"

"I *have* to do this," Sebastian insisted. Right then, it felt as though it gave him purpose in a way that nothing else could.

"It might be dangerous," Angelica pointed out. "I know you don't want to hear this, Sebastian, but we don't know what kinds of things Sophia was mixed up in. She was prepared to lie to make her way into the palace, so maybe she'd done other things."

38

Sebastian shook his head. "She was a good person."

"People do what they need to in order to survive," Angelica pointed out. "She invented a whole new identity for herself. What else might she have been forced to do to live?"

Sebastian didn't have an answer for her then. The truth was that Angelica was right. There were things that he didn't know about Sophia. He had no idea why she might have been killed, or who might have done it.

"I'll help you," Angelica said. "Whatever it takes. I might not have liked her, but I do care about you, Sebastian, and I... you know that your mother still wants us to be married?"

Sebastian didn't know what to say to that.

"She's had it announced," Angelica said. "Neither of us gets a choice about this."

"Is that what this is?" Sebastian asked. "Is this just you just trying to get control of me?"

"Is that really what you think of me?" Angelica asked.

The worst part of it was that Sebastian didn't know how to answer that. He didn't know what to think of Angelica.

"Look," she said. "Forget it for now. We need to concentrate on you. You want to find out what happened to Sophia? I'll help. Maybe I know some people you don't. Maybe I can help you put this to rest. At the very least, I can be there."

A wave of gratitude swept through Sebastian at that. He couldn't imagine anyone else offering to help him like this. He couldn't imagine anyone else even being there for him like this.

"Why are you doing all this for me?" Sebastian said. "Is it just because we're supposed to marry?"

Angelica held him out at arm's length. "I want to be there for you, Sebastian. I want this to work for us. I want—"

She didn't get to finish saying what she wanted, because at that point, a servant was there, knocking on the door with the kind of worried look that suggested that only one thing would ever force him to interrupt like this.

"What is it?" Sebastian asked, trying to be kind about it.

"It's your mother, your highness," the servant said. "She requires your presence. At once."

***

Sebastian stood outside the doors to his mother's chambers, took a breath, and pushed his way inside without waiting to be invited. On another day, he might have cared about the possible consequences of that. As it was, he just strode forward toward the spot where his mother stood looking out the window, barely bothering with a perfunctory bow as she turned.

"You summoned me, my queen?"

"Sebastian, you've returned to us." She stepped forward, saying it gently.

That caught Sebastian a little by surprise.

"You aren't angry with me?" he said with a frown.

"Oh, I'm angry," his mother said. "I'm more angry than you can believe. You walked away from your duty, from the marriage I picked out for you. You ran from your city, from your post in my army, from *me*."

Sebastian forced himself not to react. "Forgive me, my queen."

"Your queen?" she countered. "I am your *mother*, Sebastian. I did everything I could to keep you here, and you still ran away after that… that…"

"She's dead," Sebastian said. "Sophia is dead, Mother."

"Oh, Sebastian," his mother said. She took his hand and led him to the window. "It was foolish of you to go after her like that. Nothing but pain has come of it. If it were anyone else, they would find themselves imprisoned for leaving like that. Deserting your regiment when the enemy is about to invade is an offense that would see anyone else hanged."

"Then let them hang me!" Sebastian declared. Did his mother think that he cared right then? With Sophia gone, none of it mattered. If the Masked Goddess's priestesses were telling the truth, maybe it was even the one way he would get to see her again.

"You don't mean that," his mother said.

"I do." Sebastian stood there, determined not to show the pain inside him. "If they want to kill me, they can. You said that war is coming? Send me into it if you want. Throw me into the front ranks of the battle!"

His mother stared at him. He heard her sigh.

"Sebastian, why are you doing this? Why did you run off after her like that? You are a prince. You have duties."

"I loved her, Mother," Sebastian said. He didn't know how he could explain it any better than that. "You must know what that feels like. With Father—"

"This is not the time to speak about your father," his mother said. "And in any case… I did my duty. I did the things that were necessary, and so will you."

"You're talking about me marrying Angelica," Sebastian guessed. It had been what his mother had wanted even before he

40

left. It had been what she had been trying to force him to do from the start. "I know that you've had it announced. Without even asking me."

"Because this isn't about you," his mother said. She gestured to the window. "What do you see out there?"

Sebastian suspected that Rupert would have made some joke, or stormed off, but he wasn't Rupert. Whatever else was true, he wasn't like his brother.

"I see the city, Mother. I know that it is bigger than me. I know that it matters more than me, but can't I have *anything* for myself? I'm not king, and I'm never going to be. Does it matter who some second son marries?"

"Everything matters," his mother said. "But especially this. Especially *you*, Sebastian. Don't underestimate yourself. The things you do will have an impact on this kingdom, and you *will* marry Milady d'Angelica."

"To avoid making you look bad?" Sebastian shot back.

"Because the people need it!" his mother snapped. "There are enemies invading, and while our armies will push them back, it will take time. They need hope in the meantime. They need the sense that there will be a future for the kingdom. They need you to do your duty."

"I could do that on the battlefield," Sebastian suggested. "I could fight them. I could help to hold them back."

"War hasn't worked like that for a long time," his mother said. "Do you think it's about heroes trying to throw themselves into the heart of the battle? Do you think I'm going to let you kill yourself like that?"

"It's what I want!" Sebastian said.

"This isn't about what you want!" his mother snapped back. "You're going to do what you're told, Sebastian. You're going to marry Angelica. You're going to stay here and do your duty!"

Sebastian could have stormed off then, but he suspected that his mother's guards would have tried to stop him. He could have continued to argue, but he doubted that it would do any good. The truth was that he didn't have the strength for any of it anymore. With Sophia gone, there was nothing left of him to keep fighting.

He would do what his mother wanted, because what else was there?

CHAPTER NINE

Sophia watched the sea that their boat cut through, willing it to pass by quicker. How long had they been aboard now? Days, certainly, and it felt as though every one was a test of her patience. She wanted to find her uncle. She wanted to learn more about her parents.

Kate seemed to be getting even more restless. Her sister paced the ship, trying to find things to do. She didn't know enough about sailing to truly help, although she seemed to be determined to try to learn. Sophia spotted her clambering up the masts more than once, wanting to look out from the top or help with the sails.

Sophia could understand the frustration. There was little to do aboard the ship except wait, and talk, and swap stories. Sophia did her best to keep Kate entertained, telling her about her journey north with Emeline and Cora, or about how life at court had been. Kate told her about the battles she'd been a part of, talking about the violence of it all with a kind of excitement Sophia didn't think she would ever understand. Then again, she doubted that Kate was truly interested in tales of trying to fit in with the nobles at court either.

"How much longer until we make landfall?" Sophia asked Captain Borkar.

"Later today, I think," he said. "It can be unpredictable. It depends on the sea."

Sophia could see from his thoughts that he was hoping it would be sooner rather than later, the burden of having to carry two royal sisters obviously weighing on him.

"Are you starting to wish you hadn't been in the harbor when I came along?" Sophia asked.

The captain shook his head. "I would never wish that. This is a great honor. It is merely that I do not wish to be the man who sank with royalty aboard."

"*Are* we likely to sink?" Sophia asked.

The captain smiled. "I suspect that depends on how much your sister helps."

He was joking, at least Sophia hoped that he was, but even so, she pulsed out a call for Kate, hoping to drag her away from her efforts to assist with the lines of the boat.

42

"What is it?" Kate asked, running over. "Is it the baby? Are you feeling sick again?"

Sophia smiled at that. From the moment Sophia had announced that she was pregnant, Kate had fussed around her like a mother hen, seeing the least hint of seasickness or tiredness as a sign of impending disaster.

"No," Sophia said, "nothing like that, I just… wait, look!"

She pointed, Kate following the line of her finger. Even Sienne ran to the edge of the boat looking out as the water beside the boat gave way in a rush of white foam, the sleek gray form of a whale breaching the surface. It was larger than their ship, swimming alongside and keeping pace easily. Reaching out with her talents, Sophia could feel the deep, powerful intelligence of the creature as it looked them over. It swam alongside them in the water for a while before turning and diving, its tail slapping at the sea as it disappeared from sight.

There were more small islands now, some little bigger than jagged rocks sticking out of the ocean like teeth.

"In the winter, there is ice as well," Captain Borkar said. "It is part of what keeps Ishjemme safe, because only the people who know the waters dare navigate it. Don't worry, though, I know them well."

That was good to hear, and as they continued on, Sophia started to see some of the sheer beauty of this strange land. She saw distant mountains, obviously snow covered and ice filled, but behind them, the land was greener than it should have been, some trick of the mountains' protection creating a space where things could grow.

"Look," Kate said. "One of those mountains… is that smoke coming off it?"

Sophia followed the line of her pointing finger and saw it, smoke rising from a volcano in what seemed to be an endlessly swirling cloud.

"It is part of what makes the land habitable," Captain Borkar explained. "There are many hot springs thanks to the volcanoes, and the land is fertile. They say that there are slopes where a man could toss seeds and by the time he has walked away they will have sprouted."

Sophia suspected that was an exaggeration, but it did make for a spectacular landscape as their boat made its way through the mouth of one of the fjords there, the wide, craggy expanse of it leading them along the final stages of their journey. Sophia could see great bears walking along its banks, fishing in the shallows.

"Ishjemme is at the far end of the fjord," Captain Borkar said. "It is always a beautiful way to approach the city."

Sophia had to admit that was true. It was a landscape with few trees, but there were grasslands and flower meadows, and there were other things too. Someone had carved statues from the local granite, setting them along the shores so that they looked out over any vessels moving closer. Some appeared to be mythical figures, some monsters, but some...

"Kate, I'm not imagining it, am I?" Sophia asked, pointing to a statue that appeared to have very familiar features. It was of a man and a woman, and Sophia had seen them both before, in the paintings of her parents' estate.

In answer, Kate took out the locket that she carried, opening it so they could compare the features there to the ones within. There was no doubting it—the statue was of their parents.

It wasn't the only one. There were at least three more statues of them mixed in amongst the others there, while many of the remaining ones had features that suggested they were of more distant relatives. It seemed that this was a land where their family was anything but hidden, and Sophia didn't know what to think about that. No wonder the captain had been able to recognize her back at the port. If there had been more time, she might have asked to stop and look at the statues more closely, but the truth was that the chance to reach her living relatives counted for more than stone likenesses.

They rounded a bend in the fjord and now, Sophia could see a city ahead.

"It's beautiful," she said.

It was less sprawling than Ashton, smaller and seemingly more orderly, the houses built from a mixture of wood and the same stone that the statues had been carved from. Greenery was visible within the walls, in parks and gardens obviously designed to break up the unrelenting stone of the buildings. There were walls around it, intact where those of Ashton had long ago been damaged in the civil wars. Wide docks spread out in front of the city, colorful ships loading and unloading in what seemed to be a never-ending cycle of trade. Porters and wharf hands ran up to each ship as it came in to the docks, ready to help unload.

They ran in as their ship approached too. Sophia stood patiently, waiting for the ship to tie up safely. Kate and Sienne were both obviously more eager to be ashore. The forest cat leapt down almost as soon as the boat bumped against the docks, looking up as if wondering why Sophia didn't do the same. Kate hopped down

44

beside her, landing in the middle of the dock hands who were already running up to help. Sophia wasn't sure which of the two attracted more stares.

Sophia waited until the ship was safely tied up, a gangplank lowered to allow her off without having to jump. She went over to Captain Borkar, taking his hand.

"Thank you," she said. "We would never have made it here without you."

"It was my honor, your highness," he said, bowing. "If you ever need my help again, merely send word, and I will be there."

Sophia could see that he meant it, but she also found herself thinking of what it had been like trying to get his help back in Monthys.

"Just remember what I said," she said. "Help the next person who needs it, regardless of who she is."

Sophia moved down to the docks, catching up with Kate. Sienne ran to her side, obviously happy to be on dry land again. Around them, the porters were moving to the boat as if they weren't there. Sophia went up to one who seemed to be less busy, a big man who appeared to be supervising some of the others.

"Excuse me," she said, "what's the best way to get to the castle?"

"And why would you need to go there?" the man said. His accent had a kind of thickness to it, some of the sounds drawn out in places Sophia wasn't used to. "They don't let folk go just to look around, you know."

Sophia saw Kate start forward, but stopped her.

It's easier just to talk to people, Sophia pulsed across to her.

"We need to talk to Lars Skyddar," she said.

The porter stared at her, and then laughed, long and hard. Sophia could see the source of amusement in his thoughts: he thought that they were just ignorant travelers who assumed they could wander up to meet Ishjemme's ruler for their own amusement.

"Have you heard this, lads?" he called out, then switched to a language that seemed both close to the tongue of the Dowager's kingdom and a long step away from it, all at once. The men nearby laughed as well, shouting back comments that Sophia couldn't understand directly, but she could get the sense of them from their thoughts. They thought that she and Kate were fools, or adventuresses looking to snag a rich husband, or simply arrogant foreigners who thought that they could go where they wanted.

45

"Let us show you the way to a decent inn instead," the porter said. "You'll have a better time in the city than if you start bothering our ruler."

"We need to see Lars Skyddar," Sophia repeated.

"Why? What's so important that you think you need to see him and no one else?"

Sophia considered making something up, saying that she had a message, but she didn't want to start this with a lie.

"Because he is our uncle," she said.

They stared now, the porters stepping back and stopping work. Sophia could sense their confusion, and a few hints of anger from the ones who assumed they must be joking about something they shouldn't.

"My name is Sophia Danse," Sophia said, the name feeling strange even though it was hers by right. "This is my sister, Kate. Our parents are Lord Alfred and Lady Christina Danse, and I want to speak to my uncle."

She could hear the porters murmuring amongst themselves, some not believing it, some wondering aloud if it could be true. All of them looked at her and Kate with a kind of awe, either at the prospect of what was happening, or at the sheer audacity of someone willing to make a claim like that.

"Wait," the head porter said. "Turi!"

A boy ran forward, looking at them as if not quite sure what they were.

"Take a message to the castle. Tell them what has happened here. Run!"

The boy scurried off. They waited, and Sophia could feel the eyes on her. The men kept their distance, as if unsure whether they should approach or not. Around them, the business of the dock almost ground to a halt as people stopped to look at them.

"I feel like the tattooed lady in a circus," Kate muttered beside her.

Sophia might have replied, but in that moment, she saw the figures approaching. There were half a dozen guardsmen, all in dark colors, with the arms of the city on their shoulders. At their head was a woman in somber clothes that suggested officialdom. She stopped, then stared at Sophia and Kate, her eyes widening.

They look like them. The resemblance is uncanny, but... no, I have my instructions.

"You are the ones who want to speak with Duke Lars?" she asked.

Sophia nodded. "I am Sophia, and this is Kate."

46

"I've been sent to tell you that if this is some trick, some joke, you should say so now. Admit the lie, and you'll only spend a night in our lockup for wasting our time. Take it further, and there will be consequences."

"It isn't a lie," Sophia said. "Lars Skyddar is our uncle."

The woman nodded. "Then I am to take you to him. I just hope that you are who you say you are. This is not a matter for joking."

CHAPTER TEN

Around Sebastian, the preparations for his wedding surged ahead, regardless of how little he wanted them to. He wanted to be able to have time alone, to grieve properly for everything he had lost, but instead he had...

"Your highness, forgive me, but if you are not still I cannot take your measurements," the tailor said. The man had the aggrieved look of someone who already had far too many preparations to make in too short a time.

Sebastian had seen plenty of others with that look in the last day or two. There had been poets and musicians commissioned to produce the official works that would mark the occasion, servants who were to be responsible for dressing the hall, cooks who were arguing over the details of the wedding feast, and more.

Sebastian knew he was supposed to have an opinion on all of it, but the truth was that he didn't care about any of it. It felt like some great farce, where he stood still at the center of a stage while the rest of it whirled around him at comic speed. Even when he did try to engage with it, every tiny moment of it left him thinking about the wedding he should have been having instead, the proposal he'd already made, which would never be fulfilled now.

"Your highness!" the tailor said, as Sebastian stepped away.

He walked over to the window, looking out over the city. With enough height, even Ashton could look like a peaceful place, but Sebastian could imagine the battle preparations they must be making down there. He could even see a couple of them, dirt banks forming on the fringes of the city to absorb cannon fire in a way that stone walls never could.

"Is there any news on the war?" Sebastian asked, although why he hoped that a tailor would know the details of the New Army's progress, he didn't know. Maybe it was just that he felt like the least informed person in the kingdom right then, insulated from the invasion by the talk of the wedding.

"Forgive me, your highness, but your mother said that you were not to be bothered with that kind of news," the man said. "Her words were 'tell him that I have many competent generals, and that everything is in hand.'"

There was no point in asking the tailor to go against his queen's commands, but equally, Sebastian didn't like feeling useless. It reminded him too much of the way he'd felt helpless standing over Sophia's body, unable to save her; unable to even convince her sister that he hadn't been the one to kill her.

Sebastian turned as he heard the door opening, seeing Angelica enter. Today, she wore a dress of simple blue that made the blonde of her hair shine in the sunlight. It reminded him a little of the one she had worn for the ball where he had met Sophia, and just that memory sent a flash of pain through him.

"What is it?" Angelica asked, moving over to him and putting her hands on his arms. "Sebastian, are you all right?"

It was surprising that she could pick up on his pain so easily. He didn't feel close enough to be able to do the same with her, yet he could hear the concern in her voice.

"Just remembering," Sebastian said. "Your dress… it reminded me of the one you wore for the ball."

"Which was where you first met Sophia," Angelica said.

Sebastian knew he should apologize for that. He shouldn't be thinking about the woman he had loved while looking at the one he was going to marry.

"It's all right," Angelica said. "I understand that it will take time; that I'm not the one you would have chosen."

She did a good job of hiding whatever pain she felt at that, but Sebastian knew that it had to be there beneath the surface. He didn't want to hurt Angelica, especially not when she was the only one who had offered to help him find Sophia's killer.

"I'm sorry," Sebastian said. "You are… any man would be lucky to be marrying you. You're beautiful, you're intelligent, you're confident—"

"And *you're* saying it as if you're trying to convince yourself," Angelica said, with a smile. "I came because everyone was telling me that the wedding preparations would go a lot better with a groom who managed to engage with it all."

Sebastian sighed. "I don't want to spoil all of this for you. You deserve a better wedding than this."

Angelica laughed at that. "If you think that your mother will allow this wedding to be anything less than perfect, you haven't been paying attention. This is her wedding, as much as either of ours. She directs it, and we are the players, set upon the stage and expected to say our lines."

She made it sound like a duty she didn't particularly want either. But then, who would want a husband who was still mourning

49

for someone else? Sebastian knew then that he was being unfair to her. All of this was about her as well as him. They both had a duty to perform, and if Sebastian didn't do his well, then that only made it harder for Angelica to do hers.

He would do his duty then. He had no choice anyway. Sophia was gone, and he had no doubt that his mother would force him to go through with the marriage, whatever it took. Wasn't it better for everyone if he did that duty willingly? Maybe it would even help him to think about something other than the all-consuming grief that threatened to eat him from within.

"Come with me," Angelica said, holding out a hand. "All of this can wait. I had something prepared."

Sebastian frowned at that, but took her hand anyway. He let Angelica lead him through the palace, heading upward using staircases that Sebastian normally didn't use. Here and there, Sebastian saw people in military uniforms running around, obviously preparing for the coming fight.

"Ignore them for now," Angelica said. "There will be time enough for all that later. For now, I just want some time that's about the two of us. Can you do that, Sebastian?"

Sebastian knew he owed her at least that much, so he nodded. "I can try."

He let Angelica lead him up through the palace, up onto one of the flat sections of the roof, where Sebastian was surprised to see that a marquee had been set up, brightly striped and open on one side to allow them to look out over the city.

Inside, rugs were set out, along with a low table, obviously designed to allow them to sit on the floor while they ate. There were dishes set out that seemed too elaborate for just the two of them, from roast swan to candied oranges obviously brought in on ships.

"The chefs wanted us to make decisions about their ideas for the wedding feast," Angelica said, "and I thought that it might be a good chance to have some time to ourselves. To actually get to know one another."

"That... sounds like a good idea," Sebastian admitted. Already, Angelica had managed to surprise him. She clearly wasn't just the spoiled noblewoman he'd always assumed she was. She'd already proven that, so maybe he owed it to her to learn who she really was before they were married.

They sat together on the warmth of the rugs, the city spread out before them like a picture.

"I've always liked looking at the city," Angelica said. "From here, it's easy to wonder about people out there and their stories.

Thousands of things happening at any given moment, and most of them we'll never hear anything about."

"I'd always assumed that you'd find ordinary people boring," Sebastian said.

He saw Angelica shrug. "I'm not romantic about it. Most of their lives are hard and dirty, and there are plenty of criminals out there in the city. I wouldn't want to walk through the roughest parts looking for the beautiful moments. But it's nice to think that they exist. That there is *some* beauty in the world."

"I think there is," Sebastian said, looking across at her.

Angelica smiled then. "Why, my prince, was that a compliment?"

Sebastian had said it without thinking, and now guilt flashed through him at having done it. He started to apologize, but Angelica stopped him, putting a finger to his lips.

"Don't," she said. "I know this is hard for you, but it's all right to at least compliment the woman you're due to marry. In fact, I think you should compliment me again. I demand it. I demand compliments at once!"

She said that in a voice that was such a perfect version of a noblewoman making unreasonable demands of a servant that Sebastian found himself laughing despite himself.

"All right," he said, although it was hard to do this now that he was thinking about it. "You have beautiful eyes."

"It's a start," Angelica said. "You, Sebastian, are kind, and brave, and you care deeply about the things around you. If I ever manage to be loved by you, I will be very lucky indeed."

That turned Sebastian somber again. "What if it doesn't happen?" he asked. "What if we never end up loving one another?"

"Then we will try to make one another happy anyway," Angelica said. "And we will find ways for that to be enough." She reached out to touch his arm. "I do know what it's like, you know, losing someone you love."

The way she said it was enough to make Sebastian pause.

"Who was it?" he asked. "What happened?"

Angelica didn't answer for almost a minute, staring out over the city as though trying to work out if she could tell him about it. Finally, she seemed to come to a decision.

"There was a boy," she said. "His name doesn't matter. He was a minor nobleman's son whose family lived close to a house that I was staying at over the summer. You know what it's like with the tours of the oldest houses."

Sebastian did know. To escape some of the heat and stink of the city in summer, young men and women stayed in house after house around the country in a kind of slow procession of hunting parties and formal dances.

"I met him, and it was as if I'd been struck by lightning," Angelica said. "From the moment I saw him, I knew that he was the one I would spend my life with. Better, he seemed to feel the same. From the first moment we kissed, it seemed as though we were perfect for one another. I decided that I would tell my parents that I had found my future husband the moment I got home to them."

"What happened?" Sebastian asked.

Angelica laughed, briefly and bitterly. "He fell from a horse. All of that passion, all of that joy, and he fell from a horse in the middle of a hunt, trying to show off to me. Just like that, he was gone, and…" She shook her head.

"And?" Sebastian prompted.

"The rest doesn't matter. What matters is that I still feel it when I think about him. I know the pain never truly goes. I'm not expecting it to, but you can build new things too. I saw you, Sebastian, and I saw a chance to finally be happy again. Even if we don't end up deeply in love. Even if kindness and friendship is all we have."

Sebastian found himself hoping that was true.

Angelica looked over at him. "I want to try to kiss you now," she said. "Is that all right? I'm not expecting lightning, but it would be nice if there were at least something."

Sebastian hesitated, but he nodded. He would need to kiss Angelica soon enough if they were to be married.

The kiss was soft, and it was sweet. More than that, Sebastian could feel himself responding to the passion in it. Angelica was right. There was something there. It was just a question of—

"I hope I'm not interrupting."

Sebastian jerked back from the kiss so fast it almost hurt. His brother stared down at them, interrupting when nobody else would have dared. The way he looked at Angelica in particular made Sebastian want to stand up and hit him.

"What do you want, Rupert?" Sebastian demanded. Wasn't it bad enough that Rupert had dragged him all the way back here without interrupting even this?

"I know it's a pity I interrupted before you got the lovely Lady d'Angelica out of her clothes," Rupert said with a smirk that said he was picturing it. "But Mother requires our presence at once."

Sebastian could only think of one thing that would prompt that kind of urgency. The invasion had begun in earnest.

CHAPTER ELEVEN

Dowager Queen Mary stood in one of the smaller committee chambers of the Assembly of Nobles, trying to mask her impatience as she waited for her sons. Trying to mask other things too, because every moment that she waited was another in which she might find herself coughing up blood, looking weak in front of men who could not see her that way.

Even now, her physiker hovered quietly in one of the doorways, disguised only by the presence of other servants and courtiers. There were others there too, so many that they could have used the main Assembly chamber and filled it: Assembly members, minor nobles, ship captains, representatives of the surrounding towns, and of course, generals. In a land where they had more than a hundred free companies, there was a proliferation of generals.

Many of them were still arguing about pay.

"The terms proposed by the crown are simply insufficient," Sir Arthur Nallis was saying. The Dowager couldn't remember who his father was, suggesting that he was minor nobility at best.

"I agree," Charles Banquith of the Banquith Red Company said. He hadn't even had the decency to forge a family tree to claim a title, as some others might have, but his men had proved useful against some of the more rebellious factions of her kingdom in the past. "There isn't enough money to make us fight the New Army."

"The alternative is that you find yourselves killed by the New Army," the Dowager said, deciding that the moment had come to interrupt. "And then there is the matter of the Assembly's vote on the issue. Fail to show up as required, gentlemen, and you will be giving aid to the kingdom's enemies."

She didn't need to say what the penalties for that were. The Dowager sighed. There had been a time when she wouldn't have had to invoke the authority of the Assembly for this. She hoped that when their times came, her sons wouldn't find themselves endlessly mired in these arguments.

As if her thought had summoned them, Rupert and Sebastian chose that moment to enter the committee chamber, looking as though they'd barely spoken to one another on the way there. A pang of sadness shot through the Dowager at the rift that had grown between her sons. Today probably wouldn't make it better.

"Ah, my sons," the Dowager said. "So good of you to attend. We have been discussing the situation with the war." She waved a hand at one of the few generals who owed direct loyalty to the crown. "Lord Heatherwood, please sum things up for my sons."

The general stood to attention as if on a parade ground.

"Yes, Your Majesty. In the days since the New Army made landfall, it has advanced rapidly, bypassing our initial coastal defenses and destroying many of them. Already, it has taken much of the southeastern peninsula, and we anticipate it advancing north toward Ashton in the coming days. In almost every place it has passed, there has been slaughter. Those villages that have not surrendered immediately have been butchered without mercy. It currently seems to be advancing outside the town of Dathersford."

That was closer than the Dowager would have preferred, and a sudden, wracking cough reminded her that the New Army wasn't the only thing moving far more quickly than she wanted. She looked up to find the rest of the room looking back at her, and turned the cough into one designed to demand attention instead.

"Rupert, Sebastian, you have heard how difficult things are," the Dowager said to her sons. "You have both served in my armies, both shown yourselves to be capable commanders in the field. Tell me what you would do in this situation."

Rupert went first, of course. He had always been a boy in a rush, and becoming a man hadn't mellowed him.

"The only option is to counterattack," he said. "We gather a raiding force and plunge into the peninsula. There are many forests and wheat fields there, so we light fires around the enemy army, trusting the wind to carry them toward it and burn our foes. Even if it does not slay them all, an army like that will soon starve without supplies."

"A... bold option," the Dowager said. "And the fact that this plan would mean burning some of our subjects as well? The risks to the men engaged in the raid? The chances of our people starving in the wake of such a plan?"

"War carries with it risks," Rupert said, "and if people are alive behind the New Army, it is because they surrendered. They deserve to burn for that."

"I see," the Dowager said. She turned to Sebastian. "And you, Sebastian?"

Sebastian took a moment to gather himself, and the Dowager wondered if her younger son would say anything at all. Finally, he did.

55

"We should bring people in from the lands around Ashton," he said. "The city is safer than the countryside, and they can assist in building defenses here. We let the enemy come to us, and we take their momentum from them with a siege. Fewer of our people will die that way, and it buys us time."

"Time to do what?" the Dowager asked.

"Time to reach out," her son said. "We have allies, or we once did. In this we may have more. There will be plenty of people who will see this as a chance to finally defeat the New Army. We can encourage people to rise up in the lands they conquered across the Knifewater, persuade our friends to help us against them. But only if we hold out long enough."

The Dowager looked around the room, trying to gauge the reactions of the others there. Many of them were looking to her, waiting to see which option she would choose. Others seemed to be considering it, weighing up the benefits and the risks, the chances for glory and the possibilities of dying. For the moment, they were quiet, but the Dowager doubted that it would last.

"Sebastian, Rupert, you have both spoken eloquently," she said. "For now, let us leave those here to discuss your proposals. I want to speak to you both privately."

***

She led the way into an ante-chamber, leaving behind even the usual collection of servants and guards who followed her every movement. She headed over to a chair, barely making it halfway before a coughing fit took her, forcing her down to one knee.

Sebastian was there at once, of course, with Rupert there only a moment later, once he'd realized that it was the kind of thing a good son would do. There always seemed to be that slight hesitation with Rupert when it came to that kind of thing, as if he were playing a part.

"Mother, is something wrong?" Rupert asked, as the two of them more or less carried her to the chair she'd been aiming for.

The Dowager wiped her mouth, unsurprised by the blood she found there.

"Yes," she said, "something is wrong. Something I have been hiding for a long time now." There was no easy way to say any of this, so she didn't try to hold it back from them. "I'm dying."

She could see the shock on both of their faces as she told them. Good. It meant that her efforts to hide the extent of her weakness had been successful, even with her own family. If that was the case,

56

then her enemies probably wouldn't know either. Goddess knew she'd amassed enough of those over the years.

"You can't be dying," Sebastian said. "I mean… how?"

"Is it poison?" Rupert asked. Of course his mind would jump to that. "Tell me who is doing this, and I'll make them watch while I—"

"It isn't poison," the Dowager said, not wanting to hear the rest of her son's cruel imagining. "The physikers tell me that there is a cancer in my lungs that is spreading through my body. I have managed to hide its effects so far, because I did not wish to appear weak."

"Weak?" Sebastian said. "If you'd told us, then—"

"Then what would you have been able to do?" she asked. "Trust me, my boys, I have asked every doctor, wise man, and healer this kingdom has. I have asked men who have spent their lives studying the twelve books of Asclepius of ancient Hellas. I have asked priests. I even asked a would-be magician, before his execution."

She gave them a moment to consider the desperation of that, given how much time she had put into hunting down those with magical talents.

"Ultimately, they all said the same thing: there are some things that cannot be undone. I am dying, and the only thing to do is accept that fate."

She stared at her boys, then pulled them to her, holding them close. She was surprised by how much she needed that contact in that moment, but she didn't let it last too long. She had to stay strong for both of them, and for the kingdom she had worked so hard to secure.

"There are things that we need to plan," she said. "I had been hoping to deal with all this at a time of my choosing, but the invasion has shown me how little time there is."

"What needs to be planned?" Rupert asked.

The Dowager didn't hesitate. "My succession. I need to decide who will follow me."

She watched the changes in her sons' expressions. Sebastian looked surprised, but then as if he understood. Rupert mostly looked angry.

"There's nothing to plan!" he stormed. "I'm the firstborn! I am the heir by right."

The Dowager had half expected that, but it didn't make her own anger any easier to sidestep.

"If you think it works like that, then you have paid even less attention to your lessons than your tutors told me," she snapped. "Even before our house took the kingdom, it went to the one that the kingdom's magic chose." She shook her head at the stupidity of that practice, as if something as wild as magic could ever choose a good ruler. "Now, it will go to whichever person of royal blood the Assembly of Nobles acclaims."

"They will do as they are commanded!" Rupert shot back.

He still didn't understand how the kingdom worked. He didn't understand any of the compromises that had been necessary to hold onto the throne. He still thought like some potentate from days gone by, who could see his every whim obeyed. He didn't understand what it took to balance the nobles and the Church of the Masked Goddess, the interests of the merchants and the farmers, the soldiers and the rest.

"They will do as they are *persuaded* to do," she said. "And I intend to tell them that I believe Sebastian should be my heir."

"No," Rupert said. He looked as if the world were collapsing from under him. "No, you can't do that! I am the heir. I deserve to be heir!"

"Deserve?" the Dowager asked. "What do you deserve, Rupert? You are my son, and I have spent my life hoping that you would become what the kingdom needs, but the truth is that you will never be it. You are lazy. You are cruel. You make rash choices. Do you think I don't know about all the people you've hurt? Do you think no one tells me about the trouble you've caused?"

"What's the alternative?" Rupert demanded. He pointed at Sebastian. "Him?"

She turned to Sebastian. "Sebastian is wiser and kinder. Did you think it was a coincidence that I have sought a marriage for him that will bring us political allies? That I have sent him to fight our enemies? The Assembly will accept him."

Rupert stood there, so obviously angry that the Dowager suspected her son might even attack her. Instead, he turned without even the protocol of a bow.

"This isn't over," he promised, and stormed out.

CHAPTER TWELVE

Even though Sophia knew that she was telling the truth about who she was, she still felt a twinge of fear as the guards led her and Kate through the gates of Ishjemme's castle. What if their uncle didn't believe who they were? What if he treated them as imposters, out to deceive?

By the time they reached the castle's main hall, Sophia was almost trembling with the prospect of meeting her uncle. Sienne seemed to sense that fear, the forest cat looking around for enemies with every step. Even Kate seemed on edge, her hand never straying far from the hilt of the slender sword she wore.

The guards threw open the doors, and Sophia saw that what had once been some ancient hall had now been reworked as a modern grand reception room, the stone walls painted and plastered, the ceilings covered with figures out of stories Sophia only half remembered. The first of the giants, the cows Finnael had stolen from the Old Gods.

There was a throne there, but the man within did not sit on it. Instead, he had a seat set lower, behind a desk of old oak. His hair had obviously once been flame red, but was now faded and shot through with gray. His features were broad, his frame tall and slender. This was the man Sophia remembered as her uncle. This was Lars Skyddar.

She walked forward, close to the desk, trying to remember all she could, because she knew that she and Kate would have to prove who they were soon enough. She stood in front of him, trying to remember all the stories he'd told, all the things they'd done together, trying to work out which parts of it would serve as shreds of proof.

"By all the gods," their uncle said. "You look just like Christina."

He stepped forward, enfolding them both in a hug that was as all-encompassing as it was unexpected. Sophia could see the tears in his eyes as he did it.

"I never thought that we would find you," he said. "Do you remember your Uncle Lars? Sophia, I remember telling you stories, and playing at sword fights with *you*, little one." He gestured to Kate. "Looks as though you can still use a sword."

"I can," Kate said, looking surprised.

"Come, come," their uncle said. He put his arms around their shoulders. "I have so many questions. Let me show you Ishjemme."

Sophia was a little shocked by the speed with which he'd accepted them, and it was obvious that the guards were too, because they stood there a little uncertainly.

"What are you standing there for?" their uncle asked. "You think I don't know my own nieces? Go, prepare a banquet for their return! We must celebrate!"

The guards hurried off, obviously still surprised by it all. Sophia went with Kate in their uncle's wake, following him through the castle. It was a strange place, since it obviously had ancient foundations, but the interior was far more modern, reminding her a little of the palace back at Ashton.

"You must tell me what has happened to you," their uncle said. "We tried to find you after the fire, but you were gone, and we had to get your parents out of the country. What happened?"

"We ended up in one of the Houses of the Unclaimed," Sophia said. She lifted the hem of her dress, revealing the tattoo there. "We were to be indentured."

She heard her uncle's intake of breath. "A barbaric thing. Your parents sought to stop it. It is probably part of why the Flambergs wanted them dead. There was too much to lose."

"What happened that night?" Sophia asked. "I remember running, but we don't know what happened to our parents."

Their uncle shrugged. "We got them out and hid them. They've had to keep moving, though, because assassins would follow if they didn't. There are factions, even here. The last I heard, they were in the Silk Lands to the east, but that was years ago. I don't even truly know if they live."

That left Sophia feeling almost empty, because she'd been so sure that her uncle would have the answers when it came to her parents. Even so, this was more than she could ever have gotten alone.

"Come, come," their uncle said, leading the way upward, along a staircase, to a door that led out onto battlements. The air out there was cold, but not as cold as Sophia might have expected. The city beyond looked to be a place of brightly painted houses, fir trees in between them in a way that made it seem almost like a connected series of hamlets within a forest. There were walls around the city, and beyond them, Sophia could see farmland stretching out into the distance. Sophia could see some of them covered with what looked like a practicing army.

"Ah, Hans is drilling the troops," their uncle said. "He is one of my sons. He thinks that we should invade the Flambergs' stolen kingdom while they are weak and take it back."

"You sound as though you don't agree," Kate said.

He spread his hands. "I think that the ice and the mountains do a lot to keep us safe, but it is a different matter trying to invade a kingdom."

"*One* of your sons?" Sophia asked, wanting to change the subject.

Lars smiled. "I have six sons and one daughter. Come, we'll find some of them. You should meet your cousins."

He led the way back down into the castle. "Ulf and Frig will be arguing somewhere, no doubt. They live to rile one another, those two, and lately they have taken different sides over whether we should expand our borders. Ah, here we go."

He led the way into a room where two young men were playing a game with pieces shaped from dark stone. A little way away, a young woman was practicing on a harp larger than she was. All had the same red hair as their father, although the shade of it varied from bright copper in the girl to a deep auburn that was almost brown in one of the boys. They looked up as their father entered, and Sophia could feel their eyes on her.

Is this really them? the girl was thinking. *The rumors say it is, but we've been disappointed before.*

"Rika, Jan, Oli, I would like you to meet your cousins, Sophia and Kate. Girls, these are three of the small horde of my children."

The girl, Rika, came forward to take their hands. "It's so good to finally meet you. If you're staying here, I can show you around, it will be so much fun."

Jan seemed a little more reserved than his sister. Even so, he seemed pleased to meet them both, smiling as he looked over at Sophia in particular. She was surprised to find that she couldn't see his or Oli's thoughts the way she could their sister's.

Oli dropped into a bow that seemed far too serious.

"Oh, what are you doing now, Oli?" Rika asked.

The young man didn't rise. "If they are Lord Alfred and Lady Christina's daughters, then they are the rightful heirs to the throne across the water, and since the Dukedom of Ishjemme is a protectorate of that kingdom... they are our rightful rulers, Rika."

That was enough to make Sophia pause. It couldn't be right.

To her surprise, though, her uncle nodded.

"This is true, Oli," he said. "Well remembered."

He offered a bow of his own to Sophia.

"I promised your parents that you would be safe," he said. "That I would do whatever I needed to protect you. I will do that, with my life if necessary."

Sophia didn't know what to say to that. It felt as though everyone was suddenly trying to push her into a role she hadn't prepared for.

"Now," her uncle said. "We must see to that feast!"

***

Kate winced as a tattoo artist worked on her calf, obliterating the mark that had been there to claim her.

"Hold still," the man said. Kate could feel the tingle of something more than the needles as he worked.

"You have magic, don't you?" Kate asked.

The man looked up. "A little, yes. Enough that there won't be any mark when I'm done. In this place, it isn't dangerous to admit."

There was a knock at the door then, and a young man came in, looking like yet another of her cousins. He was only a little taller than she was, and was dressed in a mixture of velvet and suede broken here and there by flashes of silver.

"You must be Kate," he said. "I'm Endi. Father sent me to tell you that it is almost time for the banquet. It's good to be able to meet you at last."

"You too," Kate said, as he took her hand.

"He also said to tell you that a bird has been sent to the Silk Lands with a message. If it can find your parents, it will."

Kate dared a moment of hope at that, quickly cut short by the pain of the tattoo artist making another pass on her calf.

"Are you ready for the banquet?" Endi asked.

Kate looked over to the tattoo artist, who nodded. "I guess I am."

Her cousin frowned. "Are you sure you don't want to change first? I could have a dress brought up—"

"No," Kate said firmly. "No dresses."

She went with Endi to the hall, which was now laid out with table after table of food: fish from the surrounding waters, vegetables and herbs gathered in the hills, and reindeer herded in the lands around the city. There were many people who were probably retainers or friends of the Skyddars, but more of those there seemed to be relatives of some kind. Endi took great delight in knowing every last one of them, introducing them to Kate at bewildering speed.

62

"This is Great-Aunt Matild," he said, "and that table over there is for our second cousins who sail the fjords. Those are relatives by marriage, they don't really matter, and…"

Kate saw Sophia at a table at the head of the room, sitting with their uncle and assorted cousins. *She* had a dress, dark and lined with fox fur, looking somehow regal as she sat in front of the rest of the room. She was already laughing and talking with a pair of cousins Kate guessed to be Ulf and Frig, the young man broad-shouldered and with the barest beginnings of a beard, the young woman short-haired and looking almost as uncomfortable in a dress as Kate might have been.

Kate went up to join them, and they moved across, making room for her.

"What do you think, Kate?" Rika asked as she sat down.

"What about?" Kate replied.

"All the legends of the Silk Lands. They can't all be real, can they?"

Kate frowned at that. "What legends?"

"You haven't heard?"

"I told you," Sophia said, "the nuns didn't tell us stories of far-off lands. They probably thought it would encourage us to escape."

"It's hard to believe that anyone could be that cruel," Rika said.

Endi shook his head. "You always were soft-hearted, sister."

Frig nodded. "People always find ways to be cruel. It's why we must be strong."

"Why don't you tell us about it?" Ulf asked.

Kate did her best to explain what life had been like for them in Ashton, and that seemed to be the prompt for other stories. Oli told tales of the legendary creatures that were supposed to be common in the Silk Lands, while Jan scoffed at him for being gullible.

"The Silk Lands aren't like that," Jan said.

"And how would you know that?" his brother shot back. "The traders from there tell us about the creatures there, and the magic."

"The traders who come here tell us what they want us to hear," Jan said. "They make it sound special, so they can sell us things at twice the price."

"You're a cynic, brother."

Hans told a story about the wolves that were supposed to live out in Ishjemme's wilds, while Ulf turned that into a legend about wolves that were supposed to eat the world at the end of time. He drank mead as he told it, and so did most of the others. Even Kate tried it, the sweetness of it burning through her.

The stories kept coming, and Kate couldn't keep up with them. The truth was that it didn't matter as much as simply being at the heart of all that family, feeling as though she belonged somewhere at long last.

"Then there's the story Great-Aunt Matild tells about you and your sister," Endi said.

"A story about us?" Kate asked. That caught her a little by surprise.

"That isn't a story," Frig insisted. "It's a prophecy. You know Great-Aunt Matild used to have the family gift."

"Prophecy," Endi said with a snort. "More like a way to make the rest of us feel like we aren't keeping up."

"What prophecy?" Kate demanded.

Rika answered, reciting as if she'd learned it by rote. "Two sisters, world striding. Long ruling, life bringing. Both ruling, both standing. One by might and one by grace."

"Easy to say," Hans said, "harder to do. You're back now. Are you going to lead an army to take back the throne?"

Kate heard Rika groan. "Must we have this all the time? You and your preparations?"

"We need to be ready to take back what belongs to our cousins," Hans said. "I know Father says we must wait for Lord Alfred and Lady Christina, but if their daughters are here..."

"This is going to be your plan, to sail straight to Ashton?" Oli asked.

"It's direct," Hans said.

Kate shook her head at that. "It wouldn't work. Ashton is where the free companies gather. It's also hard to land there. It would be better to land in the north and pick up allies along the way."

"Our cousin knows strategy," Hans said with a smile.

Kate nodded. "I learned it from... from a good teacher."

She was about to explain all about Lord Cranston when something stopped her. If they did go back, she had no doubt that he and his men would be there. For all his talk of being a mercenary, he defended his home, and he followed his queen's commands. That meant that, if they did go back to Ashton, Lord Cranston would be there to fight against her.

And so, Kate realized with a leaden heart, would Will.

64

CHAPTER THIRTEEN

Endi slipped away from the feast's top table early, somewhere between Hans's second story about fighting raiders on the borders and Rika starting to talk about the nuances of harp technique. The newcomers were more interesting, because at least Endi hadn't heard their stories a hundred times, but even so, there were more useful things he could do than sit and listen to his siblings and newfound cousins.

He could listen to the rest of the family, and their retainers, for a start. There was an art to it, moving through the room the way a fish slipped through grabbing hands, never letting himself be caught in one place for too long, even though he smiled and laughed, spent a moment listening to Old Sjekar's idea of a joke, asked a distant cousin about a fishing trip.

"Harga, you old drunk, how are you?"

"Still old, still drunk. The way I like it."

On the table above, his siblings continued to fawn over the two newcomers. Oli was laughing at something the older one, Sophia, had said. Endi could see that she was beautiful, but there were many beautiful girls in Ishjemme. Typically, his family didn't go around all but giving away their holdings to them.

That was what it had meant when his father had acknowledged them without so much as asking for proof of who they were. Ishjemme might be a separate dukedom away from the Dowager's kingdom, but it was also a place that remembered the past. When the Danses had been kings and queens, Ishjemme had fallen under the cloak of their power. It would again, if Endi did nothing.

"Varli, as beautiful as ever. If that husband of yours is ever less than grateful for marrying you, you talk to me."

He kept moving through the hall, listening to the news, laughing and joking in the way he'd learned through simple practice. He'd always had a good memory, and learning to laugh with the hordes of his extended family had given him things to fill it with. He'd learned to make connections and see the truth of what was happening in Ishjemme. That had been useful more than once. For all Hans's talk of his prowess, he couldn't fight if he didn't know which roads enemies were taking.

Endi stopped by a couple of the guards. "Do you know where Bjornen is?"

They looked at one another.

"I think he's out in the northern tower, my lord," one answered. "I could send a runner."

Endi shook his head. "Don't worry about it. It's not a big thing. I lost at dice to him, that's all. Wanted to pay up."

"Now there's a man to pay your debts to," the other guard said.

Endi had to admit that was true. Bjornen the Bear was a huge man who nevertheless managed to move as quietly as a ghost, and who had no compunction about violence. Occasionally, that was useful.

"I'm not afraid," Endi said, flashing a smile, "much. I'll leave it for now."

He deliberately didn't set off in the direction of the northern watchtower, because setting off so obviously would only attract attention. Instead, he set off for the aviary where Ishjemme kept its messenger birds. Everyone who mattered was at the feast, and in any case, Endi had long since mastered the art of slipping in there without being seen. He'd been doing this for a while now.

The master of birds kept ink and long strips of paper, but that wasn't close to secure enough for Endi. He reached into a pocket, taking out a vial of clear liquid and dipping a pen into it. He started to write.

Sophia and Kate Danse have arrived in Ishjemme. LS has acknowledged. Discussion of Ishjemme invading. Acting to halt.

Endi let the hidden ink dry for a moment, then turned the paper over and scribbled a note on the other side, something brief and flirtatious, offering congratulations and asking when he might see the recipient again. He went to the corner where the correct trained birds were kept, picking out one of the strongest looking and tying the message in place. Once, the kingdom had used ravens, but with the threat posed by the Master of Crows, it had long since learned the value of doves and pigeons.

Endi carried the bird out quietly, looking around before he released it. Not that he felt shame at this. It was for the good of his land, giving information to get it, protecting Ishjemme from the threats that might have destabilized it. It was simply that he knew the rest of his family wouldn't see it that way. They would think it was a betrayal.

"Ah, sending more notes to your lover."

Endi cursed silently, then turned with a suitable look of embarrassment to face the castle's keeper of birds. The old man was as stooped and hook-nosed as any of his charges.

"You've caught me," Endi said with a broad smile. Of course, if the old man actually had caught him, Endi would have had another job for Bjornen. "Sending the most salacious details to beautiful women."

"To one beautiful woman," the old man said. "My lord, I know it is not my place, but would you mind a piece of advice?"

"I suspect I'll get it if I want it or not," Endi said with another smile.

"Find yourself a good woman here. This constant back and forth in letters may seem romantic when you're young, but a man needs a woman he can hold close."

Endi sighed. "It's easier to say that than to do it. Still, I'll think on it. And we'll keep this between us?"

He didn't insult the man by pressing a coin into his palm. Friendship was the currency the old man wanted, and would keep his loyalty better than any bribe. Endi could understand that. People wanted to be respected. One day, they would respect him as the man who had protected Ishjemme, both from outsiders and from itself. And yes, maybe the woman he wrote to would be more interested in the advances he made. She *was* beautiful, after all.

He set off through the castle, aiming for one of the small entrances that weren't well watched, a relic of earlier times, as so much else was. His brothers had talked about packing the walls with earth to protect from cannon fire, but the truth was that Ishjemme's protections were about more than stone walls.

Endi slipped out into the city, moving between the houses. He couldn't imagine anywhere more beautiful, or that felt more like home. Even in the depths of winter, when the snow lay thick on the ground, it was a comfortable, perfect-seeming place. Now, in the months before the snow came, when everything was still green, he couldn't imagine living anywhere else.

He saw people in the street and kept clear of them, where ordinarily he might have gone over to talk to them. He kept the hood of his cloak up so that the flash of his red hair wouldn't give him away if he passed too close to the light from one of the houses. He didn't mind if people around the castle thought that he was fumbling through some ill-conceived romance, but he couldn't be seen out here, not with what was coming.

It meant that it took time to get to the northern watchtower, slipping through the city, past the brightly painted homes. Endi could hear the laughter in some of them, and the music. News of the sisters' arrival must have started to filter down into the city, prompting celebration from those who couldn't see the danger in it.

"I can, though," Endi said to the darkness. It was his curse that he had to be the one to act when it came to things like this. He seemed to be the only one who understood the dangers in things that made some of his siblings cheer with joy.

How many factions were there in the city? How much had it taken to keep them balanced: the would-be invaders and the defenders, the ones who wanted to appease the Master of Crows and the ones who wanted to risk assassinating him? Endi always found the middle way, steering Ishjemme through it the way a navigator might pick out the best course for a ship's captain. Hadn't he been the one to uncover smugglers along the coast? Hadn't he dealt with traitors who might have handed Ishjemme to invaders by leading them past the natural barriers that protected it?

"This is no different," Endi told himself.

The northern watchtower lay outside the city's walls, perched on one of the hills that surrounded it. The path to it was easy enough, because the whole point of it was that messengers should be able to run back to the city if they saw trouble. Even so, the watchtowers were places that attracted men who preferred solitude, or around whom the other soldiers felt less than comfortable. Bjornen definitely fell into the second group.

Endi hurried along the path leading to the watchtower, then knocked at its reinforced door. When he heard the crunch of gravel a ways to his left, he turned, knowing that the sound was only there because the man who had made it chose to be heard.

The man who stepped onto the path towered over Endi, easily half a head taller than most men. He was broad with it, muscles barely contained by the dark uniform of Ishjemme's military. His hair and beard were graying, but that only made him look more bear-like, his eyes glittering a cold blue as they looked Endi over. In another age, he would have made a good berserker, charging into battle with no care for his safety. He even carried a short, chopping axe on his hip. Here and now, he moved through the dark with uncanny grace instead.

"Your lordship," he said, dipping his head.

"Bjornen. I expected to find you inside the tower."

"I saw someone coming up the path," the big man said. "I wanted to see who it was."

So he had gone out and stalked them the way a bear might have stalked prey. Endi wondered what might have happened to him if he hadn't proven to be... no, not a friend, because a man like this didn't have friends, but at least friendly. Probably nothing good.

"Well, it seems you've lost none of your skills," Endi said.

The big man looked almost insulted. "You thought I had?"

Endi couldn't think of anything to say that wouldn't put him in danger, so he kept quiet. That time gave him a few moments in which to consider what he was going to have to ask this man to do. It wasn't that Endi wanted to do it. He had no hatred for Sophia or Kate, no burning desire for revenge or deep sense of jealousy. It was simply that things were too carefully balanced in Ishjemme, and their presence threatened to plunge it into the kind of war that might see its quiet perfection destroyed.

"You have a task for me," Bjornen guessed. He smiled, the teeth white and hungry in the moonlight.

Endi nodded. There was no going back now.

"I do. There are people who have to die."

CHAPTER FOURTEEN

Emeline had hoped that they would find Stonehome by now. Instead, the road seemed to stretch on forever in front of her and Cora, winding away from the waterways now, into rolling lands that were prone to sudden mists and downpours.

"Are you holding up okay?" Emeline asked Cora. She could have just looked for the answer in the other young woman's mind, but she was trying to do that less with her new friend. Since Cora had no powers of her own, it would just seem like hours of walking in silence to her.

"I'm fine," Cora assured her, and to Emeline's surprise, she seemed to be. Emeline had assumed that she wouldn't be strong enough to walk all this way, finding food as they went along, stealing it where they had to. Instead, she kept up without complaint alongside Emeline, walking all day without stopping.

Emeline was surprised by that for a couple of reasons. One was that she couldn't believe someone who had lived as a servant in a palace could be used to that kind of physical exertion. The other was that she couldn't believe Cora had wanted to come with her, when she'd had the chance to go with Sophia instead.

"How much further do you think it is?" Cora asked.

Emeline shook her head. "There's no way to know. We know it's southwest, on the moors, but beyond that…"

Beyond that, they were guessing. All they could do was keep going.

They kept going, skirting villages, only occasionally passing through them when they needed to find food there or ask for more directions. Stonehome was a dangerous place to ask after though. Every time they asked, Emeline could see the suspicion in people's thoughts, trying to work out if they were witches of the kind the priestesses said should be killed for the crime of simply existing.

They got some relief from the rain in a village that had been left empty. There was no food there, because whatever there had once been had long since rotted away. Still, it gave them a chance to rest for an hour or two.

"Why do you think everyone left?" Cora asked.

Emeline shrugged. "Maybe the crops failed. Maybe there was an outbreak of plague. Maybe they were killed by raiders, or they upset the Dowager. Maybe they picked the wrong side in the civil wars."

The truth was that there were too many possible reasons a village might be empty to ever know for sure.

"So, shall we settle down for the night here?" Cora suggested. She led the way into a small cottage. "I don't know about you, but I'm tired."

The cottage was a strange place. It had the advantage of being warm and dry, and Emeline had to admit that she was tired too. Even so, she found that she didn't want to stay there. There was a sense of wrongness about the place, of there being something lurking in the background.

Then Emeline saw the faces looking back at them from the corner of the room, and she screamed, despite herself.

"What is it?" Cora asked. "What's wrong?"

"You don't see them?" Emeline asked. The forms of children stared back at her, pale and gaunt, the walls of the room visible through them. Flames seemed to flicker around them.

"See what?" Cora asked.

"I don't know what happened here," Emeline said, "but I think it was bad."

"I don't see anything," Cora said, but she sounded less certain.

"I think we need to go," she said to Cora, all but lifting her from the floor. "We'll find somewhere else to stop."

She pulled Cora from the village, not looking back.

They kept going, sticking to the road now as much as they could, passing through a forest that was stranger and wetter than any Emeline had seen before. Mist and rain looked to be constants in it, the moisture giving rise to fungi that stuck out from every tree trunk, and that rose up from the forest floor. Some were almost as tall as she was, their gills hanging down and dripping with water. There were flowers that gave off the stench of rotting flesh, while others had the sweetest perfume, and seemed to attract moths larger than Emeline's hand.

"It's strange to think that places like this can exist in the same kingdom as a city like Ashton," Cora said. "Is the whole kingdom filled with places like this that I haven't had a chance to see because I've been stuck in the palace?"

"I don't know," Emeline admitted. While she'd been stuck on the streets of Ashton, it wasn't as though she'd had a chance to explore outside it. "Maybe one day, I'll have a chance to find out. What about you?" she asked. "Have you thought about what you'll do with your life after we get to Stonehome?"

71

She saw Cora shake her head. "Not really. I was just concentrating on getting there. After that… I guess I just hoped that things would work themselves out. I guess, maybe one day, I could find work with a troupe of actors or something. I know all about makeup and clothes and things, and that way, I'd get to see what's out there."

Emeline had to admit it sounded like a good dream to have. It sounded good to have a dream that stretched ahead into the future. Her own dreams had been focused on Stonehome for so long that she'd barely thought beyond it.

They kept going, and ahead, Emeline saw a farmhouse. Since the sky was starting to darken, she headed toward it. Maybe they would be able to find space to rest in a barn, or even manage to acquire some food. At the very least, they could check that they were still heading in the right direction.

"*That* looks like a place to stop for the night," Emeline said, leading the way toward it.

"Depending on what kind of welcome we get," Cora said.

They walked up to the farm, seeing animals out in the yard. There was a horse there that looked as solid as a house. There were chickens, and even a dog.

"Hello?" Emeline called.

The door to the farmhouse opened, revealing a woman who might have been forty, with strong-looking arms and an apron coated with enough flour to make it clear that she'd been baking.

"Oh, hello," she said. "Are you lost?"

"Maybe a little," Emeline said with a smile. It was important not to seem threatening. "We're traveling south and west, trying to find a place called Stonehome. I don't suppose you've heard of it?"

"Stonehome," the older woman said. "I've heard stories of a place called that, out on the moors beyond Strand. That's a small town a little way from here. But you wouldn't be able to make it tonight. Come inside, both of you. I'm just cooking."

Emeline and Cora went inside. The interior of the farmhouse was surprisingly well furnished for somewhere so out of the way, looking as though someone had paid the costs for a merchant to bring over the finest carved chairs and tables by cart.

"Oh, this is all down to my boys," the woman said. "They travel about to trade. I'm Addie. Who are you girls?"

"I'm Emeline," Emeline said, "and this is Cora."

"It's lovely to meet you both," the woman said. "Come and sit down, and then we'll find you something to eat."

The two of them sat down, and Addie brought over bread that looked as though it had just been baked, along with stew that had the smell of mutton laced with mint and rosemary.

Come on, girls, eat up so we can get on with this.

Emeline caught those thoughts almost by accident, looking across to Cora and putting a hand gently on her arm to stop her.

"Aren't you going to eat with us?" Emeline asked.

"Oh, I ate earlier, dears," Addie said.

And in any case, it wouldn't be much good if I drugged myself.

"Well, that hardly seems fair," Emeline said. "You've gone to such trouble. Maybe we should just get off to Stonehome. It *is* where you said?"

Not that you'll get there. You're too valuable. Runaways.

"What's going on?" Cora asked. "Emeline, is everything okay?"

"No," Emeline said. "She's not planning to let us leave."

Emeline and the woman moved almost at the same time, Emeline grabbing for her small eating knife, Addie grabbing another one on the table. The older woman was, if anything, even stronger than she looked, grabbing Emeline's arms and pushing her back toward the table.

"Might as well stop struggling, girl," Addie said. "I've spent my life handling pigs and horses ever since my husband died. A little thing like you is nothing."

You'll fetch a fine price though.

Emeline struggled anyway, kicking out at her would-be captor.

"Is that all this is?" she demanded. "You snatch people and sell them?"

"You aren't anybody," the older woman said. "Probably indentured already. Certainly, nobody cares about you if you're asking about Stonehome." She pinned Emeline down, and now there was a length of rawhide in her hands. "You should be grateful. If you went to Strand asking about that place of witches, they'd probably burn you for it."

Emeline knew she couldn't let herself be tied. Cora wouldn't be able to fight off a woman like this. She was—

There was a thud as Cora picked up an iron skillet and hit the older woman. To Emeline's surprise, she hit her again, making her stumble away from Emeline. She looked as though she might hit Addie again, but Emeline pulled her toward the door.

"This way!" Emeline said. "We need to get out of here."

They ran for the door together, and it seemed that Cora's blows had slowed Addie down a little, because she was barely able to stumble after them. Emeline slammed the door shut behind them, looking around for something to block the door. Cora was already dragging over a heavy trough, pushing it in place.

"That won't hold it for long," Emeline said, already looking around for a way to escape. It seemed that Cora had an idea about that too. She was already running over to where the great horse was standing, throwing a nearby blanket across its back in lieu of a saddle.

She leapt up easily, and Emeline pulled herself up behind her. She heard a crash as Addie kicked the door open.

"Hold on," Cora said, as she kicked the horse into a run. It wasn't a fast run, but it didn't need to be. They bolted from the farm, out into the darkness, while Emeline did her best not to fall.

She wasn't sure how long they rode like that, but by the time they stopped, she was more than ready to tumble off the horse's back. She fell to her knees, gasping for breath.

"That was… we almost…"

"It's all right," Cora said, hopping down beside her and pulling her into a hug. "We escaped. We even got ourselves a new horse."

"We can't *keep* escaping," Emeline pointed out.

"We won't have to, once we reach Stonehome."

She had a point. Once they reached Stonehome, they would be safe. That meant that, burnings or not, they were going to have to find the village of Strand.

CHAPTER FIFTEEN

"No, not the cream silks, the *white*, you stupid girl!" Angelica pulled the material out of a servant's hands, tossing it aside. "Fetch something better. *Run*."

Angelica had to admit that she was enjoying the chance to prepare for her wedding. Ordinarily, she found the work of planning a ball or a party a little boring, but those were things for other people. With this, *she* would be the center of attention.

Well, her and Sebastian, but the groom hardly mattered at a wedding.

"Better," Angelica said as the girl came back with what she wanted. She patted her on the shoulder. "You see, you can do it right when you want."

She was playing nice today, and she was a little surprised to find that Sebastian was part of the reason for that. She didn't want him hearing that she was slipping into old ways, being cruel to the help. Part of it was that she didn't want to give him any reason to call this off. Part of it was just that he was Sebastian, and Angelica didn't want him disappointed with her.

Now *there* was a surprising thought.

There had been a time when the only thing that had mattered to Angelica was marrying a prince. Now, though, the fact that the prince in question was Sebastian seemed very much a bonus rather than a hindrance. Angelica tried to think about what it would be like to be married to Rupert. That thought made her shudder.

"Is everything all right, your highness?" the servant asked.

"It's still just 'my lady' for now," Angelica said, but she had to admit that she liked the sound of it. "It's Eliza, isn't it?"

"Yes, my lady." The servant looked surprised that Angelica knew her name. They often made that mistake. They thought that Angelica didn't know it, when in fact, she simply wasn't using it.

"Yes, I'm fine, thank you, Eliza."

She was more than fine. She had won the prize that she'd always wanted. Soon, she would be royal in one of the only ways that someone could become royal without being born to it. She would be close enough to the throne to touch it.

Of course, it would mean having the Dowager for a mother-in-law, but Angelica would find ways to deal with that. There were always ways to deal with even the most intractable of problems. She'd dealt with Sophia, after all.

"I just need to take a few measurements for your dress," the servant said.

Angelica stood there, letting the servant do it, but even in this, there was a difference between her and the other woman. Perhaps someone else would have stood there like a doll, moved around and manipulated to be measured. Angelica moved with grace and authority.

That was the key difference in the way the world worked. There were those with the strength of will to command, and those who obeyed out of habit. Blood could give a person some of it, knowledge more, physical strength something, but the real key was will.

"The Queen has suggested that perhaps you might like to use the mask she wore for her wedding, to demonstrate continuity," the servant said.

That wasn't all the move was designed to demonstrate, and Angelica wasn't happy about it. The Dowager was trying to remind her of her place even now. Well, she had more will than that.

"Wait here, Eliza," Angelica told the servant, deciding to demonstrate it.

The servant shifted in place, and Angelica caught her by the throat. Not hard, not enough to leave a mark, but enough to make it clear which of them was in charge.

"I did not tell you to move," she said, her voice still gentle. "Stand now. There, that's nice. Stand like that. Exactly like that. If you move even a little, I will know, and your younger sister... Masie, isn't it, will pay for it. You'll watch while she's whipped. Then I'll find an excuse to have the both of you sold."

Angelica left the servant there and went over to the desk in the corner of the room. A glance back at the servant showed her shivering in apparent fear, the need not to move only making her shake more.

It was a petty cruelty, and normally Angelica had no time for such things. If only other people were so easy to set quaking. No matter how strong she became, the memories of having to kneel before the Dowager while she threatened Angelica's life were only too fresh.

Angelica took out a ledger, opening it to go through some of the notes she kept there. The original of this had started as a diary when she was little more than a child, the whole thing in a cipher of her own devising. Over time, she had acquired many volumes, all separate. Now, each page was filled with tiny notes on every person she had met, their strengths and their weaknesses, their hopes and their dreams.

The pages for the Dowager were a complex thing of interweaving strands, most of them featuring her sons. The fact that Angelica would soon have a full hold on one of those sons was the only thing that alleviated her mood. She wouldn't be at risk in the same way when she was by Sebastian's side, joined in marriage. He wouldn't stand by and let his mother control his wife, and that would give Angelica the space she needed to do what she wished.

That brightened Angelica's mood enough that she flipped a few pages, read a brief entry, read a few notes attached to it, and went back over to the servant who stood there trying to be still.

"Thank you, Eliza, that's enough. Incidentally, there is a small house on Gutterfield Street. There is a loose brick beside the lower left lintel. You will find what you are looking for there."

"My lady?" the woman said, looking shocked.

"You know perfectly well what I'm talking about," Angelica said. "Now go please."

It was a small thing, a fragment of a favor, yet to this servant, it was everything. It was actually quite amusing to watch her scurry off looking so happy. Perhaps *this* was why Sebastian insisted on doing good for other people.

Angelica went back to her book, considering the contents even as she considered the extent of her wedding feast, the people to invite, the arrangements that would have to be made. They were all parts of the same whole, the presence of guests having as much to do with what they owed Angelica or the opportunities to bring them together as because they were friends or relatives.

There were those who might have called that cynical, but it was simply how the world worked, as far as Angelica could see. How it had always worked. Ultimately, she had a choice: she could stand there as a pawn in someone else's game, or she could play it, better than anyone else. She chose the second option.

"Now I just have to find the right moves to topple a queen," Angelica said, although the truth was that wasn't how it needed to work. She didn't need to kill the Dowager, or overthrow her, or even force her to abdicate. She just needed to create the right situations to ensure that Sebastian got power once the old hag died, and that it was real power, not the facsimile of it that the royal family had wielded for a generation.

How to do it, though…

"My lady?" a young man said, knocking at the door as he said it to drag Angelica from her thoughts.

"What is it?" she demanded. Was there some wedding preparation she had forgotten, something urgent when it came to Sebastian? Ordinarily, Angelica liked the idea of spending time around the prince who would be her husband. She had found time for meals with him, for sweet kisses that had nothing to do with the more manipulative things she'd used as weapons with others in the past. She didn't want him to see this side of her, though.

"A message has come for you by bird, my lady," the boy said. "From Ishjemme."

There were only so many people that could mean, and as Angelica held out her hand for it, she knew who it had to be. Endi, the younger son of the place's duke, whose affections she had carefully cultivated for just this reason.

Most nobles took a tour of the lands around them as they came of age. Many still did it despite the wars on the continent. Most of them wasted their time collecting mementos of the places they'd visited, rather than cultivating the kind of contacts who might tell them what was going on. Angelica had been more direct about it. She had made friends, and more than friends. She had found those who would tell her what she wanted to know for money, or friendship, or the hint of more...

She read Endi's overt message slowly, making a face. "Oh dear, I suppose I shall have to discourage this sort of thing now that I am to be married. Thank you for bringing it though."

She took out a candle, and the messenger lit it for her, obviously guessing that she meant to burn it. She did, but not before holding the paper above the flame, watching the letters that formed there in the seconds before the message caught light. Her eyes widened, and she would have read it again to be sure except that the words were already gone.

There was no mistaking what it had said, though: Sophia and her sister were in Ishjemme. Sophia was *alive*.

"No," Angelica breathed. "She can't be."

"I hope everything is all right, my lady," the messenger said, and the echo of the earlier servant's words caught at Angelica. A few minutes ago, everything had seemed perfect. Now...

...now, Angelica feared for her life. If the Dowager found out that she'd failed, that Sophia still lived, then there was no telling what the old woman might do. She might make good on her promise to have Angelica treated as a traitor, even now. She might pull apart the marriage that Angelica had worked so hard to get.

No, she wouldn't allow that. Whatever it took, and she *knew* what it would take. Endi had already hinted at it in his message. If Angelica was lucky, then there would be another message on its way already, telling her that things had been resolved. If they weren't...

Assassins were not as common as people supposed them to be. Mostly, they were madmen or fanatics, fools who could be persuaded by love or politics or religion to kill someone on the wrong side. Mostly, they died soon after. Those who killed for simple coin, and who survived to do it again, were harder to find.

Angelica flicked through her book, checking that she had it right. She wrote on a scrap of paper in a neat hand.

Sophia and Kate, in the court of Lars Skyddar. Speed is essential. Lady d'A.

She paused for a moment, and then sighed as she wrote more.

This messenger knows too much.

She sealed the paper with wax, waiting for it to cool before handing it to the messenger.

"I have a task for you," she said. "Take this to the Street of Barrels, and look for the sign of the Green Thorn. Put it into the hands of the proprietor, and no one else. Give this to him as well." She took a pouch of coins from her belt, knew that it wouldn't be enough, and removed her earrings to add to it. They had cost enough to buy a small house, but right now, there was no reason to be stingy.

So long as Sophia died, everything else was secondary.

CHAPTER SIXTEEN

They put Sophia in chambers as large as any she'd had back in Ashton's castle, with Kate somewhere nearby. Sophia half expected her sister to be in there the moment she woke, wanting to explore the city, but instead it was Rika who opened the door, coming in with a dress on her arm.

"I thought you would be up. Your sister said we should let you sleep while she rode off, but I thought that was just wasting the day."

"Kate rode off?" Sophia asked.

"Oh, not like that. Frig and Ulf were going to show her the countryside around the city."

That sounded more like Kate.

"Here," Rika said. "I brought you one of my dresses. I'll show you the city, if you like."

"I'd like that," Sophia said. It was strange how quickly her uncle's family had taken her in, and how natural it felt.

The dress was pale wool, and fit her surprisingly well. Rika led the way, showing Sophia the kitchens and the galleries, all the nooks that her uncle had no time for the day before as they headed down toward the castle gates.

To Sophia's surprise, Jan was standing by those gates, looking resplendent in a colorful tunic and a harlequin cloak. Although his thoughts were a blank to her, his sister's thoughts were anything but.

Oh dear, she really has made an impression on him.

Sophia looked across to Rika. "Um... Rika? You know that I can hear your thoughts, right?"

Normally, it wasn't something she said, but she didn't want to feel that she was eavesdropping here, and in any case, she wanted to know what Rika meant. The other girl looked a little embarrassed by that.

"I'm sorry," she said. "Father taught us how to shield our thoughts, but I must admit I was never very good at it."

"I didn't mean to embarrass you," Sophia said. "It's just... what do you mean about me making an impression on Jan?"

She doesn't know? Oh damn, she can...

"Rika?" Sophia asked.

80

"I think he's a little in love with you," Rika said, her face turning almost as red as her hair. "He's obviously trying to impress you, dressed like that."

Sophia looked across at the young man in surprise. She had to admit that he was handsome, her age, with a lean look to him that seemed more like a poet or a scholar than a warrior. She could even feel a flash of attraction looking at him.

Yet the truth was that she wasn't interested in that right now. She loved Sebastian, and the thought of anything beyond that made things far too complicated.

"Just... don't be too harsh with him?" Rika asked. "And don't tell him that you got it from me?"

"I can do that," Sophia said.

They went over, and Jan smiled.

"There you are," he said. "I heard from Rika that you'd be going down into the city. I thought I might come along, show you some of the best places."

Sophia returned his smile. "That sounds good. I really don't know much about Ishjemme."

Sophia heard Rika groan. "Don't encourage him. He'll tell you every story the skalds ever wrote."

They walked down into the city, and it took Sophia a minute or two to realize that there were no guards following along behind, no hidden watchers there to protect them, the way she'd had in Ashton when she'd been playing at being a noble. Was it really so much safer? When she mentioned it, the others laughed.

"Why would anyone need a guard to walk around their own city?" Rika asked.

"Besides, if there's trouble, we all know how to fight," Jan said, sweeping back his cloak to reveal the sword at his hip. "Father insisted."

He's not saying that he complained every time Father made him practice, Rika thought, looking away when Sophia glanced across at her.

The city was beautiful in a way that Sophia suspected Ashton had never been. There were trees everywhere she looked, so that it seemed at least as much forest as town. Wooden and stone houses sat between them, each cluster of them giving the impression of being alone in the world.

"This way," Jan said, sounding excited. "If you want to understand Ishjemme, you should see the Thing."

"The Thing?" Sophia asked.

"It's where we talk," Rika explained. "The different clans come together to discuss whatever they want, and our father can hear what they're saying. But Jan's probably more interested in the statues."

"What statues?" Sophia asked.

She got the answer to that soon enough, because on the way to it, there were carvings beside the path. Some were of people, obviously carved by a hundred different hands. Some were flat slabs with scenes worked into them that seemed to be from myth or history, or both.

"This is when Olaf Firstem fought giants for the high passes," Jan said. "They say he built himself stilts so that he could take them on face to face."

They passed by a couple of people by the side of the road. To Sophia's surprise, they bowed deeply to them. No, not to them, she realized, as she glanced at their thoughts. To her.

They said the heir to the throne had come. If this is her, then...

Jan appeared not to see it.

"This one is the battle on the drowning water, when the southerners tried to invade three hundred years ago. Nils Borsson had his men retreated across a river where they'd laid stones beneath the surface, giving them a way across that the attackers didn't know about."

"Jan likes to tell stories," Rika said. "He tells stories, Oli learns history like an old man, I sing, Hans fights, Endi knows about people, while Frig and Ulf hunt."

"Frig and Ulf *argue,*" Jan corrected his sister. "And I can fight as well as Hans."

"But I shouldn't tell him that unless he wants to test it?" Rika shot back.

Sophia guessed that Jan was trying to impress her with that. She shook her head. "I've met a lot of people who can fight," she said. "It's easy to hurt people. It's harder to give them reasons to want to work together. Stories help with that."

Jan nodded, looking happy that Sophia understood it. "This way," he said. "Anya will have finished baking by now. She makes the best sweet pastries you'll ever taste."

"I should have seen *this* detour coming," Rika said.

They stepped off the pass at a building that smelled to Sophia of fresh baked bread and pastries. There were tables set outside in the open air, and people gathered at them. They stared at Sophia as she passed. Several fell to their knees.

"I think it's going to be hard to get used to this," she said.

"That's good," Rika said. "A ruler who expects people on their knees doesn't deserve them there."

"No one deserves people kneeling just because of who their parents are," Sophia said. "This is your father's land. People shouldn't be kneeling to me."

"But in all the stories," Jan put in, "Ishjemme was a vassal of your family, under their protection. It only broke away because they no longer ruled. I would kneel to you."

To Sophia's surprise, he did just that, kneeling in front of her and holding up his sword in front of him.

"I offer you my sword, Sophia," Jan said. "I will protect you with my life. I will be there when you need me. I will stand beside you in war or peace."

Sophia looked over to Rika, hoping that Jan's sister would be able to defuse the situation with some lighthearted comment. Rika shrugged.

"I agree with Jan. I'm not much with a sword, but if you have any use for a harp player, I'll be there."

Although Jan would probably swear far more if she asked.

Sophia went to pull Jan to his feet. "If you're sworn to do anything for me, can we at least go get these pastries that you say are so good?"

"Aha, a queen who gives commands I can go along with!" Jan said.

They went inside and bought pastries from a woman in her forties who looked over her eatery with a benevolent eye. Even she curtseyed as Sophia came close, and Sophia suspected that it was only because Jan was buying that they paid at all.

When they'd eaten, they made their way down to the Thing, which turned out to be a large open space with stone terraces set into its sides. There were men there, wearing colors that probably marked out different factions or families. Some even wore plaid that reminded Sophia of the clans found in the mountain lands.

They currently seemed to be arguing.

"And *I* say that I'll not risk my family taking part in someone else's war!" a big man with a beard said.

"What if that war comes to us?" another man countered. "You think the New Army will stop at Ashton? What about if they reach Monthys? The mountains?"

"It's not our fault that you and yours chose to stay on that…" the first man said, but he stopped as Sophia, Jan, and Rika walked into the great open space there.

Sophia could feel the eyes on her then. These minds were ones she could touch, and she could feel the wide array of thoughts there, wondering about her arrival and what it would mean. Some seemed to think it meant that war was an inevitable terror. Others thought that was a good thing. Some wanted to continue being ruled by the Skyddars, while others wanted the prospect of change for its own sake.

"You've heard the news," Jan said, moving into the middle of the space. "Lord and Lady Danse's daughters, Sophia and Kate, have returned to us!"

Some of the men there bowed their heads. Some knelt briefly. Others looked at Sophia as if wondering what she might do.

"You're really her?" the big, bearded man asked. He stood over Sophia, looking her up and down. "You're the one who's meant to be our queen? Half the clans are here already, and there's more arriving every day by boat."

I've fought all my life, and I'm supposed to just obey some girl?

"I'm not looking for anyone's obedience," Sophia said, looking around at them. "And I heard you arguing before. I'm not looking for a war. I certainly don't want to invade the Dowager's kingdom in some stupid attempt to gain power."

The bigger man started to say something, but Sophia held up a hand. She knew that if she let him talk over her now, they would never listen to her.

"I'm not done," she said. "I also think that if one of you is attacked, then you all need to work together to stop them. If you don't, then when an enemy comes for you next, what help will *you* have? And don't tell me that those across the water chose to stay there. That's no kind of choice. Which of you would leave your homes willingly? Which of you wouldn't fight for them? My parents stayed until the Dowager burned it around them, until my sister and I had to run through the flames. Home matters, and we should all be prepared to work together to protect it."

She looked around, worried that she'd said too much. The men there didn't seem to be saying much. To her surprise, though, she found them nodding. Even the big man in front of her was.

"Aye," he said. "You'll do."

He knelt. He wasn't the only one. Around Sophia, man after man dropped to his knees. Even Jan did it again. Sophia looked around at Rika, who smiled.

"It seems that you have a kingdom, my queen."

84

CHAPTER SEVENTEEN

Kate laughed at the sheer freedom of riding through the hills near Ishjemme. Every time she'd been out in the countryside before, there had been a purpose to it. Now, she was just exploring, wandering for the sake of it with her cousins.

Perhaps that was part of the reason for her happiness: that she had family to share the moment with. Ulf and Frig argued with one another constantly, but Kate could see how inseparable they were, and how well the two worked together as they rode across hills and through small woods of pine trees.

"We come out here to hunt," Frig said. "Ulf might be a dullard, but he can stalk prey."

"Frig might be a loudmouth, but she knows how to track," Ulf countered.

When Kate saw the herd of elk spread out in one of the valleys below, she knew what they intended even before they asked it.

"Do *you* hunt, cousin?" Frig asked, passing across a short hunting bow tipped with horn.

"Aye, do they teach folk to use a bow back in Ashton?" Ulf put in, in between bites of an apple.

Kate smiled. "I think I may have picked up a thing or two."

Fast as only her powers would let her, she snatched the apple from Ulf's hand and tossed it into the air. She nocked an arrow and fired in one movement, skewering the apple neatly.

Frig laughed at that. "I think you'll manage. Come on."

They headed down into the valley, dismounting and moving out across the grass quickly and in silence. They kept to rocks and behind scrub, while Ulf seemed almost to sniff for the wind, keeping them in places where their scent wouldn't carry to the waiting prey.

"Does your sister have all the same talents you do?" Frig asked as she moved closer.

Kate paused, then shook her head. "Sophia can see thoughts, and... well you've seen Sienne beside her, but fighting isn't really what she's good at. She's better with people."

"People are overrated," Ulf said.

"Just because you'd sleep under a rock given the chance," Frig snapped back.

They were getting closer to the elk now, so they moved more quietly, barely making a whisper of sound as they advanced toward a stand of trees. Kate crept amongst them, readying her bow to bring down one of the creatures.

She had to bite back a shriek as Siobhan stepped from one of the trees. Or appeared to, anyway. Her supposed mentor stood before Kate, as ageless and beautiful as ever, vines entangled in her hair, her dress a thing that shimmered like the water of the fountain that was the source of her power.

"Siobhan?" Kate said. "What are you doing here?"

"I can reach anywhere *you* are, apprentice," Siobhan said. "You are mine, as surely as the land around my fountain."

"I am no one's," Kate insisted. She turned to call out to her cousins, but they were out of sight.

"Oh, don't bother calling for them," Siobhan said. "They wouldn't see me like this anyway. They might be your cousins, but *that* talent is beyond these two."

"I don't need their help with you," Kate said, trying for defiance.

"You're right," Siobhan said, her tone changing to something softer. "I'm not your enemy, Kate. I'm your teacher, and it's time to pay the price for your last lesson."

"My last lesson?" Kate said, even though she knew what it would be.

Siobhan smiled. "You saved your sister. It wasn't the lesson I intended for you to learn, but you learned it, and now you owe me. I will have a task for you soon."

Kate swallowed at that. "A task? A murder, you mean."

She thought about the last task she'd performed for the witch, about the young woman who had died at her hands in the slowest way possible because Kate had assumed that Siobhan would stop her at any moment.

"The task will be what I decide it will be," Siobhan said, in that infuriatingly calm way she had. "You know that whatever I require, the consequences will matter."

Kate could remember the lines of the future Siobhan had shown her; the images of Gertrude Illiard eventually becoming so evil that she had Sophia murdered. She still wasn't sure if she believed it.

"What game are you playing, Siobhan?" Kate asked.

She laughed at that. "Whatever game I want."

She stepped behind a tree, and Kate didn't even try to follow her. She was already gone.

The others found her a couple of minutes later, looking at her first in disappointment that she'd wandered off from the hunt, then in worry.

"What is it?" Frig asked. "What happened?"

"It's hard to explain," Kate said.

Ulf shrugged. "Try. I smell… something here."

Kate wasn't sure what to say, but if she couldn't tell her cousins this, who could she tell it to?

"Part of the reason that I'm different from my sister is because I agreed to become the apprentice to a witch," Kate said. She waited for the shock and hatred to appear on her cousins' faces, but all she saw there was sympathy.

Frig laid a hand on her shoulder. "This is not the Dowager's land," she said. "We don't burn folk for what they are. We judge them by their actions."

"What I might have to do is the problem," Kate said.

"Your witch has asked for something?" Ulf asked.

Kate nodded. "The last time she set me a task, someone died. I made a deal with her, but I will *not* just be her killer."

She saw the twins look across at one another. There was no sense of the silent conversation that might have occurred between her and Sophia, but she still suspected that they were thinking the same things. It was probably the only time Kate had seen them agree.

"For a problem like this," Frig said, "you need the rune witch."

***

It took an hour to ride to the place they were heading, Kate following behind the twins as they led the way up into the mountains, where sheer height made snow cling to the peaks and the air seemed thin.

Finally, ahead, Kate saw a place that looked as though someone had built a log cabin into the side of the mountain, so that it seemed like an awning set against it. As they got closer, Kate started to see that every inch of the wood, and most of the stone around it, was carved with symbols and runes, some looking like letters in languages she didn't know, others looking more like pictures.

"This is as far as we go," Ulf said. "People who approach Haxa must do it alone."

Frig laughed. "More like, the last time we were here, Ulf knocked over things he shouldn't have, and she was angry with him."

Kate nodded. "It's all right, I'll go in alone."

The door wasn't locked, so Kate knocked and then entered. The space beyond looked like any comfortable cabin might have, with carved wooden furniture and intricately woven throws. As with the outside, the whole of the space seemed to have been carved, in a complex web of images that seemed so detailed they could have come to life at any moment. A broad tapestry hung across the back of the room.

As Kate watched, a woman pulled that tapestry aside, providing a brief glimpse of a rock wall beyond, and of tunnels carved into that rock, presumably leading deep into the mountain. Kate found herself wondering what lay in those depths, and what would happen if she stepped past that curtain.

"I've been waiting for you. The runes said you would come."

The woman looked young, but in the same way that Siobhan looked young, as if something much older wore a young shape. Her golden hair was wild, tangled in a mess that had rune stones woven into it in spots. She wore furs and elk skins, shot through here and there with flashes of plaid, and leaving her arms bare. At least, her left arm was bare. Her right featured a rainbow's worth of colors, symbol after symbol marked there with tattoos, and even with what looked like brands.

"I'm Haxa," she said. "It's not my true name, before you ask. It just means 'witch' in one of the old tongues. And you're Kate. You should be more careful with your name. Words have power."

She extended the arm without tattoos, clasping Kate's wrist and examining it.

"You have a lot of marks on you, Kate," she said.

"*I* have a lot of marks?" Kate said.

Haxa smiled at that. "I like you. Direct as your cousins, but with enough power to be interesting. Come and sit down."

She gestured to two of the chairs, taking one. Kate sat in the other, and despite all the carving it was comfortable. There was a knife on a small table next to Haxa, and a block of wood. She picked both up and started whittling, the blade moving with surprising speed even though she didn't seem to be paying it any attention.

"You know that those with power express it in different ways?" Haxa asked.

Kate nodded. Finnael, the man who'd taught her how to heal, had said as much.

"For me, it's words," Haxa said. "Symbols, runes. I learn the names of things and their ways. I cast the runes to divine some of

88

what might come. I see the marks that others don't. You have a lot of marks on you, Kate. You have marks claiming you for another, marks of the future too, marks of power, marks of love. Which of those did you come to me about?"

"I swore to be the apprentice to someone," Kate said. "Now she wants me to kill for her."

"Then kill," Haxa said. She looked at Kate as if waiting to see her reaction.

"I won't be made to do that," Kate said.

"Ah, so it's not that you object to killing, then?" Haxa retorted. "Just to being told when to?"

Again, Kate had the sense that she was being tested. "I have killed, when I've been attacked, or when I have been defending my friends, but to be an assassin? You're right, I *don't* want to be told what to do, but a big part of that is that I know Siobhan will make me kill people who haven't done anything to earn it."

"Siobhan?" Haxa said. "The woman of the fountain?"

Kate nodded.

"A dangerous foe to have. I *should* turn you away and tell you to do what she says." Haxa looked down at what she was whittling. "But it seems that I must give you a chance."

Kate saw that she'd carved a series of small, flat ovals, each no bigger than a finger joint. They had symbols on them, angular letters that seemed suitable for carving into stone as easily as wood. She watched as Haxa tipped them into a leather bag.

"Pick one," she said. "We'll see whether I should help you or not."

Kate reached into the bag. It seemed like a foolish way to do things, relying on no more than chance.

"Don't just grab for it," Haxa said. "Feel which one calls to you."

Kate tried to do as the witch wanted, sinking into the space where she'd learned to feel for the energy of the world around her. One of the tiles seemed to feel different from the others, and Kate plucked it out.

It was blank. Haxa took it from her, staring at it, and even if she had the kind of walls Kate had come to know from witches, Kate could still tell that she was surprised.

"There were no blank tiles," Haxa said.

"What does that mean?" Kate asked.

"It means…" She nodded. "I'll help you. There may be a way to do it, even to free you, but I warn you now, it will be dangerous. This kind of unbinding… it could destroy you."

"It doesn't matter," Kate said.

Haxa looked down. "Very well, return to me at the full waxed moon, and we will see what can be done."

CHAPTER EIGHTEEN

There was, the Master of Crows had found, an art to assaulting a town or city. Foolish men charged in with siege ladders or broke against the walls like a tide. The ones who won did so by building pressure, building fear.

"Remind me of the name of this town," he said to an aide, pointing down to the town that sat below the rise where they stood, partly hidden by trees along its ridge.

"Dathersford, my lord," the man said.

He nodded. They were making progress. Sending his attention to the crows flying above revealed his forces spread out less like the army that they were and more like the beaters who might go before a hunt, driving game birds into the open for men to bring down. Instead of game birds, though, they drove people, pushing them toward the town, killing only those who strayed.

"I wonder how much longer that name will be spoken," he said.

"I do not know, my lord," his aide replied.

He looked down from the rise where he stood, taking in the city. How many lives were there within it? How many opportunities to feed the crows their due? It was a flat, old-fashioned place, encircled by walls that had probably kept out a hundred sets of raiders in the old days. There was a time when that might have looked formidable to him. Now, he knew better.

"Are the artillerists in place?" the Master of Crows asked, turning to one of his captains, Marroth. The crows told him the answer before his captain nodded, but it was still useful for men to report to him. It reminded them of their place.

"All is ready, my lord," the captain said.

The Master of Crows shook his head. "Not all. One crew is mired in the mud half a mile from where it should be. Send riders to protect them, and porters to dig them out."

"Yes, my lord," Marroth said. It was always good to see the widening eyes of those who found themselves reminded of what he could do. It told them that no plot would work, no attempt to trick him or lie.

As the captain hurried away, the Master of Crows returned his attention to the fleeing groups of peasants, harried by his men to keep them moving. Some of them ran for their lives, others trudged in lines as they tried to take their possessions with them. Idly, the Master of Crows sent one of his creatures down toward a captain of the horse, landing it on an outstretched arm.

"There are peasants to the west moving too slowly," he had the beast croak. "They have carts of food. Take the carts, drive the peasants on."

Food was as important a weapon in war as any cannon or sword. Drive enough people into a town before a siege, and it would not be able to feed itself. There were other uses for them too.

"Here they come," he said to the men around him. "Be ready."

Around him, the men of his army stood, preparing for what was to come, moving with the discipline that came from knowing that failure would be punished.

Now, the fleeing peasants came into view, running in disorganized waves of humanity, hurrying across the ground before the city. The Master of Crows could feel the tension rising amongst his men, obviously eager to begin their work.

"Wait," he commanded, watching, letting the first fleeing figures reach the town's open gates. "Now."

His men surged past him, down onto the flat ground before the city. They moved in a sea of ochre uniforms, covering the ground with the controlled speed of fighting men rather than the panic of the fleeing.

Even so, they quickly caught up with the slowest, their blades beginning the grim work. The screams carried over it in a way they probably would not have in a true battle. There was no musket fire to drown them out, no clash of steel on steel, only the dying of the weak and the roars of the bloodthirsty.

In the distance, beyond the violence, the Master of Crows saw the gates to the city starting to close.

"The city's leader is foolish," the Master of Crows observed. "He should have closed the gates days ago to keep out hungry mouths. He should have closed them the moment he knew we were coming."

Not that it would have made much of a difference. Gates could be dealt with. For now, those of Dathersford slammed shut, the sound of it ringing out with the finality of a tomb door closing. Some of those the New Army had sent running had made it inside. More still stood out on the plain before the town, shut out from it as surely as the Master of Crows' men were. Some ran, some struck at the gates with their fists, a few even tried to climb the walls.

The Master of Crows' army fell on them and slaughtered them, men, women, and children. They cut them down as they ran, or begged, or even tried to fight. There was no mercy.

"Bring the spikes, and load the cannon," the Master of Crows said.

His captains hurried to obey. For his part, the Master of Crows set off on a slow walk across the battlefield, strolling through it as calmly as if he'd been wandering along a promenade. There were screams and moans from those who were merely wounded rather than finished, their cacophony adding to the sight of mangled flesh and the stench of death.

The Master of Crows stopped outside the walls, where his aides were already setting up impaling spikes. As he watched, they dragged a couple of the wounded peasants toward them, ignoring their screams.

"Please," a woman begged. "I've done nothing to you. You don't need to do this. Show some mercy!"

The Master of Crows regarded her impassively. "And what good would mercy do? What fear would it bring?"

He listened to the wounded scream while his men executed them.

Only once they were done did he turn back to the city. Its walls were lined with men now, still little more than a rabble, although with a few more fighting men amongst them than the villages had held. It was the way of things: men kept their armies close to them, not wasting them on those further away.

The Master of Crows gestured, and horns blared.

"I will give you three choices," he said, his voice carrying with echoes as every crow in the city repeated it. "The first is to surrender now. If you do that, you will lose nothing but your freedom. This city will become mine, and you will continue your lives. You have one turn of the glass to decide."

Very deliberately, he had one brought forward, his men turning it.

"We're safe behind our walls!" a fat man in the rich clothes of a merchant called back. "I'm the mayor of this town, and Dathersford will not surrender to you! We have stood through war before. You do not scare us."

"As you wish," the Master of Crows said. Even so, he waited the full turn of the glass, letting those within have time in which to watch the writhing agony of those on the impaling spikes, giving them time in which to see the ones that still stood empty.

Finally, the last grains of sand ran out, and the gates were not open. He turned to Marroth. "Begin."

Trumpets blared to give the first signal, and artillery roared in response. Cannon blared with the kind of power that had once belonged only to sorcerers. Mortars threw stones up to fall within the city. Muskets sounded, firing at anyone foolish enough to keep their heads above the parapets once it began.

Walls that had stood through centuries of previous violence cracked and crumbled as cannonballs struck them. The gates that had slammed closed so defiantly turned into things composed of splinters that jabbed at those beyond. The New Army tore the protections from the city as surely as a servant taking away an unwanted cloak.

Finally, the Master of Crows held up a hand. The bombardment ceased almost instantly, leaving silence that only seemed greater for the noise that had gone before. He spoke again, and again, his words were carried by the crows.

"Your first choice is gone to you, but you have two more. You can surrender now, or you can fight on. If you surrender, you will lose a little. One-third of the city will be taken as slaves, while your leaders will be executed. My men will have one day of looting before they leave. That is the price of not surrendering at once. If you fight... not one soul within the city will be spared. No two bricks will stand together. Dathersford will cease to be."

Very deliberately, he turned the glass again.

He waited, standing still even as his men started to move into position to begin their assault on the town. They set themselves near the breaches, but also brought the cannon around to bring down the rest of the walls if required.

The sands were almost gone by the time the small delegation came through the gates, visibly shaking. The fat man who had called down his defiance was at their head, his hands bound behind him as some of the city's guards shoved him along with a coterie of others.

"These are the leaders of the city," one of the men said. "We wish to accept... we want to accept your offer."

The Master of Crows smiled, gesturing for his men to move forward.

"Tell the men that they have one day," he said to his aides. "And get the slave lines marching back to the boats. After that, we need to be ready to move again."

"Yes, my lord," Marroth said.

Behind him, the Master of Crows heard the screams as the executions began. He smiled at that, knowing how much the fear would do when they finally got to Ashton.

Soon enough, it would be the Dowager on a spike, and her kingdom would be his.

CHAPTER NINETEEN

Sophia stood by Ishjemme's docks, staring out in the hope that one of the incoming ships would bear good news. She watched as ships and smaller boats came and went, hoping each time one pulled up to the docks that it would bring with it the one message she wanted to hear:

Sebastian was coming for her.

She'd started by looking out from the castle's walls, but that hadn't been enough for her. What if Sebastian came and found himself turned away, or was even attacked as one of Ishjemme's enemies? Sophia couldn't stand for that to happen, so now, each day, she came and stood by the docks, waiting and hoping.

Briefly, she saw a young man whose broad shoulders reminded her of Sebastian, and she found herself starting forward without even thinking about it. Then the young man turned and Sophia saw that his features were too round, his beard a full thing that had no place in her memories. She stepped back again with a sigh.

Beside her, Sienne pressed against her leg to comfort her. The forest cat went everywhere in the city with her, looking around with a mix of curiosity and superiority that only a cat could manage, and leaving her side only to snatch fish heads from passing fishing vessels.

"Are you *still* waiting for Sebastian?" Kate asked.

While Sophia had spent her days wandering around the city, enjoying learning about her uncle's home with the aid of Rika, Jan, Endi, and Oli, Kate had mostly spent her time beyond the walls with Frig and Ulf. She had hunted with them while Sophia had spent her time learning about the different clans of the dukedom, and had toured defenses while Sophia had spent her time trying to learn a few fragments of the local dialect and understand the alliances that Ishjemme had built.

"He'll come," Sophia said, knowing that Sebastian would follow if he could. She had to believe that. Her fingers found the ring he'd given her. That had to mean something, didn't it?

"If he comes, they'll announce him at the castle, in the warm," Kate said. She didn't sound as though she really believed he would be following.

96

"It's not just Sebastian," Sophia said. "There might be news of our parents."

"Because you sent a message," Kate said. She sounded as though she wasn't any more hopeful about that, although she also sounded as though she wanted to be.

If we can find them, we will, Sophia sent across to her.

It doesn't mean we should be waiting on the docks, Kate sent back. *They want to talk to you at the castle about allies, and diplomacy, and...*

"And other things you're too busy hunting to bother with?" Sophia guessed.

"Not just hunting," Kate said, and for a moment, her expression was serious. I found someone in the hills who..."

What? Sophia sent. *Don't leave me waiting for you to finish.*

"News! News from the Dowager's kingdom!" a sailor called out. It was enough to distract Sophia instantly from the question of whom her sister might have met.

"What news?" Sophia asked, turning toward the man with all the speed that hope could muster. She reached out with her powers, hoping to see the answers even before she heard them. When she did, she all but staggered with it, mouthing her disbelief even before the sailor had said it.

"They say that Prince Sebastian is to marry Milady d'Angelica in an effort to rally the hopes of the kingdom," the man said. "They say—"

"I'm pretty sure we don't want to hear any more of what they're saying," Kate said beside Sophia. She put a hand on her shoulder, and Sophia could feel her there, steadying her, holding her up. "Go and tell it at the castle."

Another time, Sophia might have called her out on her rudeness, but right then, it felt as though she didn't have the breath for it. Her heart felt like it might explode with the pain that wrapped around it, and she felt sick in a way that had nothing to do with the usual rigors of pregnancy.

"He can't," she said, shaking her head. "He *can't*. It must be a mistake."

"You saw it in his thoughts," Kate said. "The news is all over Ashton. It's real, Sophia."

Her sister hugged her, helping her from the edge of the docks to a crate that Sophia could at least use as a seat. Sophia was grateful for that, because otherwise, she suspected she might collapse from the sheer shock of it.

"Not her, though," Sophia said. "Anyone but her."

She didn't mean that. She didn't want anyone marrying Sebastian at all. She wanted him running to her, speeding his way across the intervening sea using whatever ship he could hire, commandeer, or steal. She wanted him there declaring his love, not getting married. If he had to, though... not Angelica. The choice of *her* seemed almost calculated to hurt, because she was everything that Sophia wasn't, everything that a prince was supposed to want.

"You had to know that he would do this," Kate said. "I met him, remember. He wants to play the part of the dutiful lover, but he gave me a ring for you rather than follow you himself, and then he was standing over you with a knife..."

"That was Angelica!" Sophia insisted. It came out louder than she intended.

"I know you believe that," Kate said. "But I also know what I saw." Sophia saw her shake her head. "Maybe it was both of them. This marriage... it says to me that they might have been in it together. Maybe it was a way of making sure that their marriage could work."

Sophia couldn't believe that. She *wouldn't* believe it. Sebastian wouldn't do something like that, and it had definitely been Angelica wielding the knife. Right then, that almost didn't matter, because the news of the wedding hurt almost more than the knife had.

"You need to forget about him," Kate said.

"I can't," Sophia insisted.

"You know it's the right thing to do." Kate ruffled Sienne's ears, but to Sophia's surprise, the forest cat growled softly. "Hey there, Sienne, do you not want me to do that, or do you just not want me upsetting Sophia?"

If you know it's upsetting me, Sophia sent, *why say it?*

"Because sometimes we have to do things that hurt now, because we know that they'll be good for us later. Like with Sebastian. I guess it was probably wonderful being in love with him, but I *know* it's hurting you now. Maybe a little more pain now is worth it if it stops more in the future."

It isn't just a little more pain, Sophia sent. She didn't feel as though she had the strength to speak words aloud right then. Besides, it meant that she could let Kate feel some of what she felt, the raw anguish that came with learning about the wedding.

That's what I mean, Kate sent back. *He's already hurt you so much.*

That's not Sebastian, Sophia insisted. *It's just...*

"It's everything around him," Kate said. "It's the fact that his parents had ours murdered. It's the part where he has an evil brother

98

who thinks the world is his plaything. It's the part where he cast you out, then toyed with your feelings by coming after you, then went to his new bride. It's whatever role he played in trying to kill you!"

"He didn't do that," Sophia said again.

"But all the rest is still true," Kate pointed out. "If we're who we are, then we're his enemies by default. Loving him will only make that harder."

"Or maybe loving him is what a situation like this needs," Sophia countered.

Even so, it hurt. Finding out that Sebastian was going to marry Angelica felt like the biggest betrayal there could be. How could he do a thing like that?

"Come on," Kate said, reaching out to put an arm around her. "We'll get you back to the castle, and then… well, I'll get the twins to keep an eye on you. I have to get ready to do something."

On another occasion, Sophia might have asked what, but right then, it felt as if the world were collapsing in on her. She pulled away from her sister.

"I'll be all right," she said. "You go do the things you need to do. I'll get back to the castle by myself."

I don't want to just abandon you, Kate sent, but at the same time, Sophia could sense that whatever her sister had planned, she wanted to do it almost more than anything.

"I'll be fine," Sophia said, even though she felt she would be anything but fine right then.

She watched Kate hurrying off, obviously consumed with whatever this thing was that she had to do. She stood there, trying to look strong and untouched by the news, even though she felt she might shatter at any moment, like cracked glass in the cold.

She kept wondering how Sebastian could do it, and there was only one answer that she could think of: he thought that she was dead. There was a kind of protection in that, in the world beyond Ishjemme not knowing about her, but if it also created a place where Sebastian could marry Angelica, Sophia didn't want any part of it.

She had to find a way to let him know that she was alive.

She made her way to the castle, and from there, it only took a little asking to find the place where the messenger birds were kept. They squawked in their cages at the sight of Sienne by Sophia's side, and the noise of it pulled their keeper from the half slumber that he was in.

"My lady…" the man said. "I never thought… your animal, is it watching me?"

In fact, Sienne seemed to be watching the birds as if wondering why so many snacks were in one place. Sophia calmed her with a pulse of her gift.

"I need to send a message," she said. "And I need to make sure that it reaches Prince Sebastian. Not his mother, not one of the people who might tear it up, but Sebastian. Is that possible?"

The master of birds considered it. "You could send a note with a messenger," he said, "but if you wish to use a bird, the best that can be done is a sealed message, marked for him alone."

It would have to be enough. Sophia took a quill and parchment, setting down her message in small script and hoping that *this* time, Sebastian would receive it.

Sebastian, I love you. I am alive, and in Ishjemme. I am carrying our child. Please, if you love me at all, come to me. Sophia.

There was something about writing a message for a bird that reduced even the most important thoughts to brief, incomplete things. As Sophia sealed the message and wrote Sebastian's name on the outside, then lifted the bird and let it fly, she could only hope that it would be enough.

CHAPTER TWENTY

Lord Cranston was drunker than he should be, but that seemed to have become the norm in the preceding days. It was a poor Free Company that couldn't find wine when it needed it, and he had taken full advantage. It helped to numb some of the feelings of loss.

"My lord," an adjutant said, "a royal official has arrived. The same messenger before, and he's smiling in a way I really don't like."

"Thank you Kate, I'll be along directly." Lord Cranston realized too late what he'd just said. "Damn it."

"Possibly better not to mention that name in front of the queen's man, sir," his adjutant said.

"I know that," Lord Cranston said. "Go see if you can slow him down. I should at least try to look presentable."

"Yes sir," the man said. He put a flask on the table. "The cook said to drink this. That it never fails."

"Thank you," Lord Cranston said. If they were resorting to homemade recipes to sober a man up, things truly were getting desperate. "You may go."

The man saluted, and Lord Cranston waited until he'd gone before standing unsteadily. It was hard sometimes to see how far you'd let yourself fall until someone pointed it out. He'd been this way...

Well, that was easy enough to pinpoint. He'd been this way since Kate left.

He'd told her not to. He'd *ordered* her not to, and the fact that she'd gone anyway had been more than bad enough. Yet the truth was that this wasn't about anger at being disobeyed. He could even admire the bravery it took to row away, stealing a boat like that and cutting herself off from all the people who might have protected her.

"I miss her," Lord Cranston said. On impulse, he drank down the cook's concoction. It tasted every bit as bad as he felt right then. He straightened his clothes and walked out from his tent, into the camp.

The men were training hard there, working with weapons, drilling formations. Almost automatically, Lord Cranston sought out the spot where the boy Will was working with the cannon crew, moving woodenly, as if he didn't care. He was probably the only one there more hurt by Kate's departure than Lord Cranston was.

Lord Cranston had lost more than enough in Kate. She'd been such a brilliant student, and she'd saved all of them in the battle at the New Army's harbor. She'd been like the daughter Lord Cranston had never had, an apprentice worthy of following in his footsteps, and now she was gone.

Lord Cranston saw the queen's messenger standing ahead, delayed by his men but looking more impatient by the moment. On impulse, Lord Cranston turned away from the man, setting off through the camp. Let the messenger chase him for a while.

"News, lads," he called out. "Someone tell me the news."

His sergeants came up. Harris, who handled the training of raw recruits. Berrus, who ran the artillery. The quartermaster and the cook followed, because there were some things at least as important to a company as its fighting strength.

"Who wants to go first?" Lord Cranston asked.

"They're saying that the New Army has taken Dathersford," Harris said. Lord Cranston had heard that part already. "They have enough men to fight in a dozen spots at once, and they are. Every time a force tries to sneak in on them, or get around them, there they are."

Lord Cranston nodded at that. He could believe it after what had happened on the beach. If the man genuinely could see through the eyes of his crows, then tricking him would be nearly impossible.

"It's pretty dire," the quartermaster said. "I've heard stories from the farmers who bring in the food to the queen's men. They've been pushed back, mile by mile. Half the time, they aren't even bothering to defend anymore. And food prices are going up too."

Lord Cranston knew that was more than just the griping of a man who had to find the coin to pay for it. Food prices were going up because of the land being taken by the enemy, because of the refugees running ahead of them, and because the queen's forces were taking what there was.

It suggested that this was a long way from simply repulsing a few raiders. They were losing this war, and the effects were starting to show.

"There are other rumors," Berrus said. "A man I get powder from does business over in Ishjemme. The stories say that Kate is there. In the castle."

"*Our* Kate?" Lord Cranston asked. "What did she do? Try to assault it single-handed?"

It sounded like the kind of thing that she might do. Even so, Berrus was already shaking his head.

"No sir. They say that she and her sister... they're the Danses' daughters. They're *royalty*."

That was a phrase that might get a man hanged in another context, but around him, Lord Cranston's men knew that they were safe.

"Have you mentioned this to young Will?" Lord Cranston asked.

Berrus shook his head. "No sir."

"See that you don't. Not until I work out what to do with news like that. You're *sure* it's her?"

The other man nodded, as Lord Cranston had guessed he would. Even so, it seemed incredible that Kate, the girl who had escaped from the House of the Unclaimed, should turn out to be someone on whose existence whole countries might turn.

"Say nothing for now," Lord Cranston said. He glanced back toward the messenger. "Especially not to our friend there."

He could see the man looking over, his anger palpable. There was no putting off the need to go and talk to him any longer, so Lord Cranston marched over, trying to look as composed and worthy of respect as he could. He wouldn't be cowed by the fact that this man served the Dowager.

"Ah, hello again," Lord Cranston said. "So soon after the last time that we met."

It was designed to be deliberately disconcerting, and honestly, maybe it had a little to do with the drink, as well. Still, the messenger managed to maintain his composure.

"My lord," he said. "You have kept me waiting intolerably."

"Only as the needs of my company have required, I assure you," Lord Cranston said, sweeping a hand around the camp. "As you can see, we take the preparations for war very seriously."

"And its execution as well," the messenger said. "My mistress, your queen, would like to congratulate you on your successes against the New Army."

"And yet I am not summoned to the palace to receive a medal," Lord Cranston observed. What was it about this man that irritated him to indiscretion? It didn't matter. What mattered was that he wouldn't be here without a reason. "What is it that our beloved Dowager requires of me and my company?"

The other man looked at him, stony-faced, then took out a letter. "Commands from the palace. Your free company is to travel south to hold the bridges over the Sessert River, between Ashton and Dathersford. Upon receiving further instructions, it will advance to engage the enemy, as part of a coordinated strike with others of your ilk to drive back the foes. You will receive further instructions once you are in position."

Further instructions? They would have to be good ones, because the current set seemed to be simply to move forward to fight the New Army in the open. It was madness, because even if it somehow succeeded, even if the Master of Crows didn't outmaneuver them, it would mean losses for the companies on a scale that was impossible to contemplate.

"Is the plan to simply throw paid men at the enemy in the hope that you don't have to pay them when they die?" Lord Cranston demanded. It was impolitic, but it was a suicide mission on a scale at least as great as the attack on the docks had been, and this time, Kate wasn't there to save them.

"It is not my place, or yours, to question our queen's plans," the messenger said. "These orders have come from the palace, and your company has already been requisitioned under lawful orders signed by the Assembly of Nobles. To fail to obey would be treason."

Lord Cranston might have been drinking, but he was still sober enough to notice the fine detail in that. This wasn't something that had specifically been agreed with the Assembly then. Nor, now he thought about it, had the man said that the queen herself had commanded this.

The trouble was, despite all of that, the man was correct. The free companies had been called up for the war, the mandate of the Assembly unequivocal, and disobeying now would put all his men at risk.

All or some; it hardly seemed like a good choice, but it was the kind of choice a commander had to make. Of course, the best found other ways; ways that made a mockery of the choices put to them by others.

"When do we need to be in place by?" Lord Cranston asked, trying to stall for enough time to find that third way.

The messenger smiled. He was enjoying this, damn him. "You told me before that your company could move in mere hours if you commanded it. Give the order now, please, Lord Cranston. Or should I tell my superiors that you refuse to obey?"

He had said as much, and now he was paying the price. Lord Cranston looked around, seeing his men there, some still training, more staring at him. They might not be able to hear every word of this, but they must know what was going on. It was impossible not to. What could he do other than give the order, though?

What would Kate do in a situation like this? Lord Cranston smiled at that, because now he had his plan.

"Men," he called out. "Form up and prepare to strike camp. We need to be ready to march. I'm taking you to Ishjemme!"

There was a moment of shocked silence, and then Lord Cranston heard the cheers starting at the back of the ranks. In spite of his orders, it seemed that more than a few knew what was waiting for them there.

"But..." the messenger began, "... you can't do this. It's *treason*. I'll see you hang for this. I'll—"

Lord Cranston struck him then, barely more than a push that sent him sprawling.

"You'll go back to your masters, and tell them that Lord Cranston's company is unavailable for their war. That it will be going to seek an engagement with rulers it actually *respects*. That Lord Cranston wishes you all luck in trying to win without our help. Now, I think you should go, don't you?"

The other man scrambled to his feet, seemed to think about striking back at Lord Cranston, and obviously thought better of it. Lord Cranston waited for the man to go, then turned to his troops.

"Pack your things, boys, and be ready to move. We're going to serve Kate and her sister, and I doubt the Dowager will like it much!"

CHAPTER TWENTY ONE

Sebastian was more nervous than he'd thought he would be, even given that it was his wedding day. His stomach was aflutter with the thought of it, and just trying to imagine standing beside Angelica, swearing his vows before the Masked Goddess, set his heart racing.

"Is there anything that still needs to be done?" Sebastian asked. "Are there any preparations still to be made?"

The servants around him shook their heads. Some even looked mildly insulted that he would ask.

"Everything is in order, your highness," a valet said. "The Dowager is seeing to the preparations herself."

Probably driving Angelica mad by doing it. The wedding had seemed like a battle between the two of them from the beginning. Even that battle seemed preferable to standing there while everyone else fussed around him. It seemed as though there was nothing more useless than a prince on his wedding day.

"The people have turned out in droves, your highness," the valet went on. "I imagine for many of them it will be the biggest event of their lives."

Sebastian went over to the window, looking out over the city. There was indeed a sea of people spread out in the streets, and to his surprise, there didn't seem to be guards herding them into position. He'd been half expecting his mother to make people celebrate, forcing them to under threat of incurring her displeasure.

"The people out there," he said. "They do *want* to be there?"

"Of course they do, your highness," the valet said. "Why would you doubt it?"

Sebastian fixed him with a level stare. "What's your name?"

"Moore, your highness."

"Well, Moore, can we assume for a moment that I'm not an idiot? People talk about how beloved my family is, but that's just something my family's supporters say."

"I couldn't comment, your highness," the man said. Sebastian had the sense of a man caught in a dilemma, unable to comment without the prospect of being heard by the other servants.

"Don't worry," Sebastian said. "I'm not going to make you say something that could get you dismissed, but those people out there... they aren't being paid to be there?"

"No, your highness," Moore said.

"Or forced, or herded into place by the guards?" Sebastian pressed.

The man shook his head. "If I were to guess, your highness, I would say that it is because they love you and Milady d'Angelica. They think you are a beautiful couple, and they are hoping to be distracted from the news of the war."

Sebastian swallowed at the thought of being the main distraction for so many people. Of course, soon he would be a lot closer to them, because his mother had arranged for him and Angelica to ride through the city in one of the royal carriages, making sure that they would be seen by as many of the people as possible.

"Are you *sure* that there is nothing for me to do?" Sebastian asked. "There must be all kinds of things that still need to be done."

"Certainly, your highness," the valet said. "But I was explicitly told that you weren't to be—"

Sebastian set off through the palace, hoping to find something that could take his mind off the wedding nerves. He wasn't surprised to find that, the moment he stepped out of his rooms, the palace was alive with servants working on every aspect of the wedding preparations.

There were men and women carrying food and setting up decorations, turning the palace into a confection of gold and silver that seemed like something out of a dream. A whole team of servants with dusters and cloths were cleaning every surface they could find, while more were trying to find places to entertain guests who had arrived far too early. It reminded Sebastian a little of the preparations for the banquet that seemed like a lifetime ago, only this was a hundred times more complex.

"I shouldn't be thinking about that," Sebastian told himself. Thoughts of the banquet brought with them thoughts of Sophia, and those were thoughts he shouldn't be having on his wedding day. "Think of Angelica."

He would have gone to find her if he could have, but the tradition was not to see a bride in the hours before her wedding. Once the veil of the goddess went on, she ceased to be the person she had been, and it was the worst of luck to so much as glimpse her before the wedding.

Sebastian wandered the halls of the palace, because even just walking was better than standing there being fussed over. He went down to the galleries that showed the kings and queens of the past, seeking out the family portraits, the pictures of strong-looking men standing beside beautiful women, trying to imagine himself and Angelica standing like that while someone painted them. Perhaps Laurette van Klet would agree to it.

"Prince Sebastian," a servant called. Sebastian turned, seeing a young man hurrying toward him. "Prince Sebastian, I've been sent to find you."

"Let me guess," Sebastian said, "I'm supposed to come back so that they can make the perfect wedding mask for me, or make sure that my outfit has no wrinkles?" On another day, he might have complained about the sheer performance of it all. Today was Angelica's day, though, and he wasn't going to ruin that for her. He was going to be the best husband he could be. "I'll be along right away."

"It's not the wedding," the young man said. "There... there's a bird for you."

"A bird for me?" Sebastian said. That was a rarity. Messages came and went, of course, because a palace like this one was automatically a hub for communications of all kinds. There were messengers carrying sealed packets and those who had simply memorized what had to be said. There were letters sent with anyone going in the right direction. There were even bird messages for the palace, or for his mother. A bird meant specifically for Sebastian was a rarity, though.

"It had your name marked on the message, sealed against tampering," the servant said. "The bird was sent from Ishjemme."

"Ishjemme?" Sebastian asked. He couldn't believe it. That was where the ship carrying Sophia had been heading before... before she died. Just the thought of that made his throat catch. "You're sure?"

"I know it sounds strange," the young man said. "But I checked in the ledger we keep of birds so that we don't send them to the wrong places. This one was definitely from Ishjemme."

Sebastian didn't know what it might be, whether it would be Kate writing to berate him or threaten him for what she saw as his role in her sister's death, or the captain of the ship writing to tell him what had become of Sophia. Maybe Kate had even found herself needing to use his name if she'd found herself in trouble there. At a minimum, Sebastian owed it to her to help if he could.

"Show me this message," he said.

The servant nodded, and then set off through the palace. Sebastian hurried after him, hoping he wouldn't be seen as he did it. Even though there was nothing wrong in anything he was doing, he suspected that Angelica or his mother wouldn't be happy to hear about it. Even Rupert would find a way to make trouble if he learned about Sebastian receiving secret messages.

Sebastian made his way through the palace to the high atrium that housed the aviary. There were birds from around the world there, ready to fly at a moment's notice, even if it was more reliable to put a message into someone's hands. There were brightly colored birds from the Near Colonies, along with doves and crows, ravens and more. A cage housing a single dove sat on a rough wooden table, a message set out before it while its occupant rested.

"Is that the one?" Sebastian asked, and when the servant nodded, he snatched up the message, breaking the seal in a rush. When he read what was written there, he all but staggered back from the table.

Sebastian, I love you. I am alive, and in Ishjemme. I am carrying our child. Please, if you love me at all, come to me. Sophia.

There were so few words there, yet they felt as though they broke something open inside of Sebastian. For several seconds, he could only stand there, staring down at the message, unable to comprehend it.

"Your highness, are you all right?" the servant asked.

Sebastian didn't answer, just hurried from the room, seeking a way out of there and into safety. He all but ran past servants who called to him, wanting to know if they could help. He ignored them, making his way up onto the palace's roof, leaning against the balustrade at its edge and trying to remember how to breathe properly.

"She's alive," Sebastian said, because maybe hearing it would make it more real. "Sophia is alive!"

He heard the last word turn into a sob and felt the hot sting of tears as they fell. Right then, he couldn't tell if they were tears of happiness or guilt or sadness or relief. Sebastian could feel his emotions tangled up in a knot inside him, the threads twisting and turning so that they made no sense.

Sophia was alive, which meant that he'd abandoned her without checking thoroughly enough, and that he'd wasted his best chance to be with her. Sophia was alive, which meant that all the grief that had threatened to consume him was for nothing.

More than that, Sophia was pregnant.

The first part of it had been so huge that it had all but obscured the second. Now, though, the thought of it filled Sebastian. Sophia was pregnant, with his child. She was alive in a foreign land, and was about to become a mother. The joy of it tangled with fear for her and how things might go for her traveling alone there, even with her sister to protect her. Sebastian wanted to run to her in that moment, to be with her. He wanted to wrap his arms around her as he should have a long time ago and promise never to let her go.

"Your highness?" Moore the valet was up there on the roof now, his expression featuring the harassed look of a man who had been looking everywhere without success. "The servants said that I would find you up here. It's more commonly the bride who gets wedding jitters."

Sebastian wanted to tell the other man to leave him alone. He wanted to shout the truth about Sophia to the heavens, yet he didn't, because the awful reality of it hit him then. Sophia was alive, and at the same time, he was promised to another. He'd pledged himself to Angelica, and in just a little while...

"I'm sorry, your highness," Moore said, "but you really do need to come back inside. From the look of your outfit, you'll have to change, and there isn't much time before the procession around the city. It's almost time for the wedding."

Almost time for the wedding. To Sebastian, it sounded like a death sentence.

CHAPTER TWENTY TWO

Prince Rupert looked around the small meeting room in the Assembly of Nobles, trying not to show any of the contempt he felt at having to persuade people rather than simply order them, maintaining the smiles and the joviality that seemed to convince so many people to do the things he wanted.

He'd learned that lesson long ago—that people were stupid, and didn't look beyond the surface of things. That if you looked good, and you smiled, and you pretended to some interest in their pitiful lives, then they would not just obey, but hurry to do it as if they were doing you some great service.

"Are we all assembled?" he asked, checking who was there and who was not. Lord Birly, Sir Quentin Mires, and Earl Stutely were all there, along with a collection of lesser men. Sir Henry Carramire was absent, Rupert noted, in spite of his invitation.

The man would have to die for that, of course. There was no question about that. It wasn't just to ensure that no one talked about what he was proposing. There was also the matter of ensuring that there would be no chance of men disobeying him again. Rupert would teach the world its place, even if it seemed to have done its best to forget it.

"Your highness," Admiral Meers said. "What is this about?"

He sounded almost impatient. Not the tone to take with his prince. Then again, Rupert had heard that the man had lost almost half his ships to the enemy by now. Perhaps he had good reasons to feel a little out of sorts.

"It is about the war, Admiral," Rupert said. "What else *would* it be about?"

Rupert had instructed a servant to bring a map of the island and spread it out for them. He gestured the way he imagined a commander might. Usually, he left that side of things to others.

"You have all heard the reports. The New Army is continuing its advance, filling our southeastern peninsula and taking the towns there. The cowards are surrendering to them now, rather than risk fighting them."

"Because those who fight are slaughtered," General Sir Launceston Graves said.

"At least they die without giving in to our enemies," Rupert said, banging his fist down on the table. "They reduce the numbers of our foes, rather than going over to their side. They fight for their rulers, as subjects should!"

His tutors had made him read the histories and the plays of the past. Rupert had found most of it boring, but he had liked the moments when great men had given speeches. He had liked the idea that, with nothing more than a few words, someone of the right blood could manipulate others into fighting and dying for him.

"The situation is grave indeed," Lord Birly said. "Yet what can we do? The army's plans have been set. We are to wait in Ashton, building defenses, drawing the enemy to us."

"A different brand of cowardice," Rupert said. "And one I'm sure you brave men have no wish to engage in."

He looked around them one by one. Any man who argued now would be branding himself a coward in the eyes of those around him. Rupert was quite proud of that, and he left it another few seconds just to sink in properly. He understood how to get obedience.

"What if I told you that I had a better plan?" Rupert said. "What if I told you that with enough boldness, we could stop this invasion, destroy our foes, and secure the glory of victory?"

"I'm sure that we would be eager to hear such a plan, your highness," Earl Stutely said, in the kind of diplomatic tone that made Rupert want to do something drastic just to see if anything would make him be impolitic. Perhaps he could seduce the man's wife, or find a reason to seize one of his estates.

Rupert looked around at them. Now was the moment; the kind of moment that great men seized and lesser men allowed to slip by. Rupert had always been good at seizing moments, whether it was with women, or on the hunt, or in killing those who opposed him. He had the kind of decisiveness that other men lacked, the ruthlessness to do what was needed in the moment that it was needed.

"Earlier," he said, "instructions were sent from the palace to the commanders of the Free Companies employed in the war. They have been moved forward, away from Ashton, and to points forming a cordon around the peninsula. On the morrow, they will receive orders sending them forward."

He left that a moment for the shock to set in. He even enjoyed that moment. There was nothing quite like the look on someone's face when they realized that they'd underestimated what he was willing to do.

He wasn't done though.

"Your troops, gentlemen, will replace them. You will form a ring of steel around the peninsula, and you will make it into a ring of fire. While the paid men move in like a sword thrust, you will be the crushing vise and burning brand, moving in behind them and leaving nothing in your wake."

"Nothing, your highness?" Lord Birly asked. Rupert had long wondered about the squeamishness of others. They balked at doing things that seemed so obvious to him, so natural.

"You will burn crops, fields, and villages," he said. "You will leave nothing for the enemy to make use of. You will set fires whenever the wind will drive them deeper into the peninsula, cleansing it the way a surgeon might cauterize a wound. You will kill anyone who is not carrying our fighting colors."

"Anyone, your highness?" Admiral Meers said. "The common folk—"

"The common folk will have either been killed already or have betrayed us by surrendering," Rupert said. "If we kill those who try to run, it will persuade the others to rise up and fight for their homes, as they should have done in the first place!"

He waited to see if anyone would argue with that. They didn't, because Rupert had chosen the men at this meeting carefully. He'd picked men from the factions who saw themselves as natural superiors to the common folk, and who wanted to preserve things the way they'd always been. Such men might manage a kind of paternal benevolence toward the poor, but when it came to it, they recognized that there would always been more peasants.

"What about the Free Companies?" Admiral Meers insisted.

"They will be moving forward to engage the enemy. If you meet them, urge them forward. If they refuse, or you catch them running, they are to be treated as deserters."

It was a move that would both push them into a desperate assault and ensure that the power of the Free Companies was reduced afterward. A clever man could make use of what was left of them, absorbing them into the royal army, building it up.

Rupert could see the men around the room looking at one another, hear the whispers as they started to consider it. Sometimes all it took was for men to see the possibilities in an idea.

"It could work," Admiral Meers said.

"It's a bold stroke," Earl Stutely said.

Rupert could see them coming around to it, as the weak always did in the face of the strong. They *were* weak, in spite of their elevated ranks. They saw themselves as grand men, but they were as foothills before a mountain. They *would* do this. Still, he had to anticipate objections. He *had* anticipated them, his answers already tucked away like knives sharpened for use.

Lord Birly asked the first question. "What will the Assembly of Nobles say to this?"

"I think they will say thank you," Rupert replied. "I think they will realize that they were about to have an army descend on these meeting chambers, and that they have been saved from it. I think that, by the time they hear about this, it will already be in motion."

"And they will not object to that?" Sir Quentin Mires asked. He'd been quiet until now, but his brother was a member of the Assembly. "They will not feel that the crown has overstepped the bounds of the settlement with it?"

Rupert longed for the days of the distant past, when a ruler could simply ignore such objections. When a man who spoke against its decisions was a traitor or a seditionist, fit only for the gallows. Now a man, even one in line for the throne, could do nothing without the support of the nobles.

"The Assembly has voted to give the crown its support in the war," Rupert said. "It cannot hope to oversee every detail of its execution, or our enemies will be on us before the first meeting is concluded. I'm sure that you see that, Sir Quentin."

He saw the nobleman nod.

"All of that is true, your highness. Even so…"

Rupert forced a smile. "I'm trusting you and your brother to help us deal with the 'even so's,'" he said. "Or has your faction in the Assembly come to doubt me?"

"Certainly not, your highness," Sir Quentin said. "We are loyal servants of the crown, even if others forget their role."

He undoubtedly meant it. He and his kind had a kind of loyalty bred into them, the way hunting hounds might have. It wasn't something Rupert had ever felt, but he could understand it well enough to make use of it.

"Speaking of the crown," Earl Stutely said. "What will your mother say to this, your highness? I was under the impression that she favored the more… defensive approach your brother advocated."

Rupert could have struck him for that, but he didn't. He knew enough not to strike a man when there was a chance of it harming his own efforts.

"There are those," Sir Quentin agreed, "who might see this whole meeting as suspicious. Powerful men meeting behind closed doors, to subvert the stated will of the Dowager? We all have enemies who would be happy to see us disgraced for this, even beheaded."

Rupert smiled, because he'd been expecting that worry as well.

"I'm perfectly aware of the potential consequences," he said, "but I will deal with any problems. I can handle my brother, and my mother."

"How, exactly?" Earl Stutely asked.

Rupert shook his head. "Just leave it to me," he insisted. "I am your queen's eldest son. I am the man who has a way to deal with this war. I am the one you should be *listening* to. If we do this, we will be the men who saved this country. We will be the men who defeated the New Army. But I'm told that a prince cannot simply give orders. This is a place of votes, so we'll have a show of hands. Who is with me?"

Rupert looked around, watching them raise their hands one by one. He wanted to see if there was anyone else who had to die. He wanted to see who was loyal. Under the weight of his gaze, they all lifted their hands, all declared their part in it.

"Very well," he said. "It's decided."

And now that it was decided, everything else could start to fall into place.

CHAPTER TWENTY THREE

When she saw the first of the stone circles, Cora knew that they were getting closer to Stonehome. She could feel her excitement building at the prospect, and she could only guess at how happy Emeline must feel in that moment.

"We're almost there," Emeline said. "Stonehome can't be far now."

The stones stuck up to about the height of her waist, worn almost to nothing by the wind and the rain. Even so, Cora found herself wondering who might have done a thing like that, and why. Beyond them, a moor spread out in a wash of brown and green, peat and moss that stretched most of the way to the horizon. More stone circles stood here and there, along with outcrops of rock that seemed almost like islands sticking up from it.

There was a town closer to them, butting up against the edge of the moor the way a port have with the sea. Cora guessed that it was Strand. She couldn't see the one thing she wanted to.

"Shouldn't we be able to see Stonehome?" she asked.

"I don't know," Emeline admitted. She looked worried. "I'd hoped that we would just *know* or something, once we got here. Hold on."

Her face creased in concentration for a moment, and Cora guessed that she was using her gift. Since there was no one there to talk to, Cora suspected that Emeline was doing the mental equivalent of shouting "hello" at the top of her voice.

"Nothing," Emeline said, and Cora could hear the disappointment there. She knew what it meant, and she knew that she was going to have to be the one to suggest it.

"We're going to have to go down into the town," Cora said.

"People are dangerous," Emeline replied. "Look at what happened when we stopped at the farm."

Cora could understand her worry. It felt as though they were about to make the same mistake they had before, but what other choice did they have?

"We'll be careful," she said. "We won't even *mention* Stonehome. We'll just be two travelers passing through, and you can watch out for any sign of it while we do it. Maybe we can buy a map, pretending that we're on the road to somewhere else."

Emeline looked doubtful, but even so, she nodded.

They walked down into the town. It was a small place, with the feeling that it was only a town rather than a village because a couple of larger roads converged on it. As she walked in, Cora could see a marketplace where people were selling vegetables, cloth, freshly cut peat, and what looked like carved stones harvested from the moors.

There were enough travelers and merchants there that people didn't stare at them as they came into town. It made a nice change for Cora. Since she'd left the palace, it seemed that everyone they met had been suspicious of them. She was able to relax a little, looking around at the market stalls and wondering if they had enough money to buy what they needed.

She didn't mention Stonehome. Instead, Cora chatted with stallholders about the weather and the road south.

"What brings you down this way?" one merchant asked.

"I've family that lives further along," Cora said, knowing by now the lies that would deflect attention most effectively. "We only stopped here because of the market, and the chance to hear the news."

The merchant shook his head. "Not a lot of good news going about these days. The war hasn't spread here yet, but it's still making it hard for merchants. If you have family around here, better to take them and go north."

"That was the plan," Cora lied.

She kept up the pretense as she moved around the market with Emeline. They were down here to see their family. They were cousins. They weren't staying long. All the while, Emeline stayed near, presumably looking out for any sign of Stonehome in the minds of those around them, maybe even calling to see if anyone would reply. Their plan seemed to be working.

Then Cora saw the stakes.

They were set apart from the rest of the market, iron things that rose up from the earth, spreads of sand around them showing the space where a fire might be set, or blood might be absorbed. They were the kind of thing that might see people tied to them to have their debt sold on, or for a whipping, but those weren't the things that Cora thought of when she saw them. She thought of the way the iron would heat with flames at its base, and how wood might be piled high around someone as they stood.

This was a place where they burned those with gifts.

Cora was still thinking about that when she saw the priestess. Actually, there were three, and they moved through the marketplace in concert, their veils and robes rendering them almost indistinguishable. There was only one, though, whose head turned toward Cora and Emeline. Cora might not have Emeline's gifts, but she had spent enough time around the more predatory sort of nobles to know when someone's attention was not a good thing to have.

She tapped Emeline on the shoulder. "I think we need to leave."

Emeline followed her gaze, and then nodded. "Slowly though. I don't think they've seen us yet."

For Cora, the hardest part was trying to hold her nerve, trying to be as casual as she had been when walking into the small town. She needed it to look as though she had just changed her mind about going to the market, and—

"Witch!" the priestess cried out, one finger jabbing like a broken branch in their direction. "Catch the witches!"

"Run!" Cora yelled to Emeline, setting off as fast as she was able.

They dodged through the crowd, Cora pushing aside a woman with a basket full of washing, so that clothes and blankets went everywhere. She shoved past a bulky man, setting him tumbling into another.

It was still in the space of a chase where no one had quite worked out what was happening. They needed to gain some distance as quickly as they could, because already, Cora could see people starting to work out that they should be acting. One made a grab for her, and Cora barely broke free of his grasp. She saw another man grab hold of Emeline, and Cora spun to her, pushing the man away so that the two of them could start running again.

They darted down an alley, the crowd following after them. Cora sped up.

The journey had given her strength that she hadn't known she possessed before. She ran, and for a brief moment, she and Emeline were alone, with no one following. Cora looked around, trying to find anything that might help them.

"What happened?" she asked. "We didn't mention Stonehome, but that priestess—"

"I felt her," Emeline explained. "She's been trained."

Cora tried to ignore just how frightened her friend looked at that prospect.

"I don't know what that means," Cora said.

"They're taught by the Masked Goddess's church to hunt the rest of us," Emeline said. "Maybe they had flickers of talents themselves as children, or maybe it's just their training. They can sense when we touch their minds, and I've been shouting to anyone who will listen."

Cora kept looking around. Life in the palace had taught her to be able to find places to hide with only the slightest notice. Servants weren't supposed to be seen, and those that were could quickly find themselves punished for it. Now, they had seconds at most.

"There," she said, pointing to a space where a house had a cellar whose doors opened onto the street. There was a trapdoor above it, and she quickly hauled that open. Within, the smell of drying peat was almost overwhelming, but Cora pulled Emeline down into it anyway.

"You don't understand," Emeline said, but Cora held a finger to her lips. They needed to be silent.

Outside, she could hear the sounds of their pursuers. There were shouts now, and there was even the barking of dogs, although Cora doubted that any dogs would be able to smell them over the thick, earthy scent of the peat they rested in. She kept her head low, daring to put an eye to the thin crack between the two doors that let in sunlight.

There was an eye staring back at her.

"They're in here!" the priestess called.

The doors above Cora were thrown open, and she found herself surrounded by townsfolk. She flung herself forward, ready to run again, but this time the surrounding crowd was ready for her. They grabbed at her arms, pinning her in place as securely as if they'd tied her. Cora looked around, hoping that Emeline might be able to help her to break free, but the townsfolk had her as well.

Cora fought, but fighting did nothing. There were so many people that they were more like a force of nature than a collection of individuals. Even when she felt her foot connect with a man's leg, it just earned her a punch in return.

They dragged her in front of the priestess and her companions, forcing Cora to her knees beside Emeline.

"You are a witch," the priestess said, staring at Emeline. "I heard you calling, searching for Stonehome."

Beside Cora, Emeline said nothing.

"Silence will not save you," the priestess said.

Cora laughed at that. "You're going to pretend that something will? You're going to lie to us and tell us that there's some way that you let us go?"

The priestess turned to her. "You are not a witch. You do not have the stink of their vileness. Yet you travel with one, you aid her, and you seek Stonehome."

"Emeline is my friend," Cora shot back. "She has helped me ever since I got out of the..." She trailed off, realizing that this wouldn't be a good moment to mention the palace, or Rupert. She would rather burn to death than be given back to him.

"Since you got out of where?" the priestess asked. She reached out, pulling up the hem of Cora's dress, revealing the mask tattoo there. "You have fled the goddess's price. You deserve to be punished just for that."

Cora saw her look to the others.

"The Masked Goddess is merciful, though," the priestess said. "Denounce your friend as the witch she is. Agree to work in one of the temples of the goddess. You will be spared."

"Do it," Emeline said. "Save yourself, Cora."

Cora shook her head. "If that's your idea of mercy, I don't want it. I'd rather die free."

The priestess stepped back as if Cora had slapped her.

"Very well," she said. "You can burn beside the witch."

CHAPTER TWENTY FOUR

For Kate, the hardest part of getting to Haxa the rune witch's home was doing it without her cousins coming with her. If Ulf or Frig saw her leaving, they would undoubtedly want to come too, to try to help or simply to be there to support her. Kate suspected that this was something she had to do alone.

So she made her way out of Ishjemme quietly before going up into the surrounding hills. She could remember the path from her previous trip, even though it felt different here, like this. Just the thought of what she was going there to do made the hills seem more on edge, echoing with the threat of a storm.

Kate kept going. She needed to do this.

It wasn't long before she made it to Haxa's cabin. Kate paused, swallowing as she tried to fight back the sudden nerves that had started to build up inside her. This moment had the potential to set her free, but Kate had felt the kind of power Siobhan possessed. Kate doubted she would be set free from it easily. Maybe it would be better not to risk it, especially now. Maybe it would be better to turn back.

That would mean doing whatever Siobhan demanded of her next. Kate couldn't do that. She couldn't kill another innocent person. Raising her hand, she knocked on the door.

"Come in, Kate," Haxa called from inside. "Everything is set up."

Kate walked in, but she couldn't see any difference in the house compared to the last time she'd been there. The walls were still the intricately carved artworks that Kate remembered, the furniture was all in exactly the same position. Haxa sat at one side of a small table, runes set out in front of her. The curtain at the back of the cabin was closed, covering over the way deeper into the hillside.

"I wasn't sure if you would come," Haxa said. "Runes and names have their power, but they are not able to predict things precisely. I trusted that you might, though."

Kate looked at her. It would have been easier if she had been able to read the witch's mind. She could have worked out what she might gain from this, and why she was doing this.

"You don't trust me," Haxa said.

Kate wasn't sure what she could say to that without lying.

"I do not take that as an insult," Haxa said. "There is a good reason I do not give people my name. I do not trust them with it. Most would never harm me, but they would still say it carelessly, and it would reach those who might. This is not a world for trust."

"But you have still offered to help me," Kate said, "without asking for anything."

Haxa nodded. "And you do not trust that. Well, that is your choice to make. Come with me, or don't. I won't try to force you."

She stood and went over to the curtain, pulling it aside to reveal the cave mouth that stood beyond. Where it had been dark the last time Kate had been there, now it glowed faintly with a light that hinted at something brighter, hidden within the depths of the mountain.

"All right," Kate said. She didn't want to sound afraid, even though she was. "I'll come and look."

She followed Haxa down into the depths beneath the hill. The rune witch drew out a small stub of candle, setting it glowing to provide yet more light as they walked, and by it, Kate could see carvings worked into the walls at least as intricately as in the cabin. There were letters in a dozen alphabets, ranging from runes to pictograms, with lines of flowing script in between that looked as though it would have been nearly impossible to carve with a chisel.

Then there were the pictures. Kate stared at them as they went lower. There were pictures of faces and of strange creatures, far-off places and objects that Kate couldn't begin to guess at the uses for. Each was accompanied by a series of letters in a simple carved oval. Somehow, Kate knew that those letters represented names, and not just ordinary names.

"If you want to learn to read them," Haxa said, "*that* will cost you."

Kate shook her head. "I don't think I want to be another witch's apprentice."

Haxa smiled. "And I have no patience for teaching. But I will help you with this."

She continued to lead the way through the tunnels. There were branches to the left and right, turning the place into a web of corridors that Kate knew she would have been lost in instantly had she been alone. Haxa led her unerringly, though, down to a spot where the light grew stronger, and the corridor started to open out.

The room beyond the cave didn't have walls carved with scenes or faces, just with letter after letter, set in lines that seemed almost like the bars of a cage to Kate, there to contain power, or channel it. They ran in perfect circles around the room, while more circles sat on the floor, this time in widely spaced lines that looked like the concentric walls around some ancient castle.

A plinth sat at the center, and on it, Haxa had set a stone cup, again carved with so many stylized letters that it seemed almost to be something alive.

"What is all this?" Kate asked.

"The right words have power," Haxa said. "Names have power. This is a place where that power can be worked with, explored... even changed."

"You're going to change my name?" Kate asked, not understanding.

Haxa looked at her for several seconds. "I guess that *is* one way to put it, but no, I am not literally going to rename you. It is more complex than that."

Kate stared at the seemingly endless runes spread around the perimeter of the cave. "How much more complex?"

Life was easier when she could fight her way through her problems. Give her an enemy to battle or a friend to save, and Kate could do it. She'd proven that again and again, in her return to the House of the Unclaimed, on the battlefield, even with Siobhan's specters. Moments like this, when there was magic involved with rules, she couldn't begin to understand.

"There is a connection between you and Siobhan," Haxa said. "In becoming her apprentice, you changed things about yourself, you forged a link that is a part of who you are now."

"And you have the means to break that link?" Kate asked.

Haxa shrugged. "Not exactly. I am not strong enough to go up against something like her directly, especially not with someone she has claimed so strongly."

"I am *not* hers!" Kate insisted.

Haxa put a hand on her shoulder, the weight of it probably meant to be reassuring. Her next words weren't, though. "You are. It is written into the fabric of your being."

Kate started to pull back, but Haxa's grip was stronger than it looked.

"What is written can be unwritten. If you drink from that cup, it will not wash the words away, but it will give you a chance to do it for yourself, if you are strong enough."

"If I'm strong enough?" Kate echoed.

Again, she had the sense of things she didn't understand.

"You are going to be making changes at the level of your very being," Haxa said. "That is never easy, and with something like

123

that... it will fight back. It will not be easy. There is a chance that everything you are could unravel."

That made her sound more like a piece of cloth than a real person, and made what could happen sound far gentler than it would be. Kate understood what the witch was saying, though. If this went wrong, she could die.

Then there was Siobhan's anger to consider. She wouldn't have the same connection to Kate, wouldn't have the same power over her as she'd had before, but she would be angry about that loss. She would go from being an ally to an enemy in an instant, and a dangerous one at that.

"No," Kate told herself. "She was always an enemy."

"What's that?" Haxa asked.

Kate shook her head. "It doesn't matter. Tell me, what would I have to do?"

Haxa gestured to the cup. "Step over the lines of runes, being careful not to touch any of them. Drink from the cup. After that, I can't tell you what it will be like."

"We experience it differently," Kate said, thinking of what Finnael the healer had told her.

"Exactly," Haxa replied. "All I can tell you is that you must find whatever changes Siobhan has wrought in you and find a way to cut them clear. If you manage to do it, you will no longer be hers. She will no longer have a claim on you if you do not wish to do what she asks."

"And what do you get out of this?" Kate asked. She'd tried to ask it before. Maybe this time, Haxa would answer her.

"Siobhan is powerful, with the way she manipulates things," Haxa said. "I have no wish to see a thing like her in control of life and death."

"And would I find myself controlled by you instead?" Kate asked. "You said that names have power. How much of mine would you see?"

Haxa nodded. "A good question, but I swear to you this: I am not trying to control you. It is not *you* I'm interested in."

"And I won't be stuck owing you someone's life?" Kate asked. She wasn't going to make the same mistakes again.

"No," Haxa said. "Given all they say you're destined to do, I suspect that your gratitude will be more than enough repayment. That is all I can tell you. So now choose, Kate. Will you do this thing, or do you want to walk away?"

It was that simple, wasn't it? For all the considerations that went into it—the danger, the threat of Siobhan seeking revenge, the task that Siobhan wanted her to complete—it just came down to that choice. Kate could do this, or she could turn back.

It was her choice, though, and that mattered. If she didn't do this, then she would never truly have choices, because Siobhan would always be there in the background, trying to control her.

She stepped forward, grabbed the chalice, and drank it down in one long swallow. For a moment, the world seemed to tilt, but a second later, everything seemed normal again.

"Now what?" she said, turning to Haxa.

At least, Kate started to turn. Halfway around, it seemed more like it was the room that was turning, spinning so that the runes there spun with it, becoming blurred things that left afterimages on her vision. Kate blinked, trying to make sense of them, but they burned on the inside of her eyelids now, spinning faster and faster, building into something that seemed to pulse to the rhythm of her own heartbeat.

Then that pulse stopped, and Kate felt her legs give way as the floor came up to meet her.

CHAPTER TWENTY FIVE

Sebastian stood waiting for his wedding. On the outside, he probably looked still and calm—no worse than a groom should look on his wedding day, at least. Inside, he was roiling, the news that had come in shaking through him the way an earth tremor might have.

Sophia was alive.

"Is everything all right, your highness?" a servant asked him. A whole contingent of them surrounded him, fussing over him in a way that felt like a team of squires strapping some ancient knight into his armor.

"I'm fine," Sebastian lied, because what else could he do at this point?

Trumpets sounded, heralding the moment when he had to go through with this. The servants all but herded him forward. Perhaps they thought that it was only natural for a man to be nervous on his wedding day. Perhaps they were under orders from his mother to make sure that it all went ahead without a problem. None of them would dare to go against his mother.

Or Angelica.

"The wedding mask, your highness," a servant said, holding out a blank white mask, meant to symbolize all the roles that he played as an unmarried man. Sebastian took it, slipping it into place. When he and Angelica faced one another, they would remove each other's masks. Only at the end would they give one another new masks to wear.

"Are the new wedding masks ready?" Sebastian asked, sudden nerves striking him.

"Constructed by the finest mask-makers of the city, your highness," the servant said, in tones obviously carefully calculated to soothe.

As he walked toward the doors to the grand ballroom, Sebastian tried to concentrate on the bride he would be marrying in just a short time. He tried to focus on the fact that she was beautiful and clever, that she was the right match for the kingdom, that she seemed to see into his heart more than he'd thought she would. She'd even shown a more sensitive, less demanding side to herself since the wedding announcement.

Even so, every thought of Angelica morphed into one of Sophia, until Sebastian couldn't pick their faces apart in his thoughts. Even as he tried to concentrate on the woman he would be marrying, he found himself wondering about what things would be like for Sophia in Ishjemme, and if she was safe.

"The people are filling the city in celebration," the servant said. "They want to be a part of this moment."

Sebastian moved to a window, looking out. By now, there were so many people on the streets that it was hard to take them all in. There were fires set at regular intervals, suggesting that someone, probably Angelica, had arranged for them to have the chance to keep warm as the sun set.

The doors to the grand ballroom swung open, showing half of the nobles of the realm in neat rows, all dressed in the kind of finery that only they could manage. The room was awash with finest cloths of purple and gold, silks and velvet. The guests were arranged by rank, Sebastian guessed, so that the finest and richest garments found themselves clustered toward the front, where an altar to the Masked Goddess had been set up, and her high priestess stood waiting.

Sebastian felt all of their eyes upon him as he began the slow walk toward his appointed place. His mother's eyes were foremost among them. Queen Mary of the House of Flamberg sat on a throne to one side of the proceedings, too important to sit with the masses even of the noble houses, yet not, for once, the center of events.

"Behold Sebastian of the House of Flamberg," a junior priestess announced, while the high priestess waited by the altar. "Beloved of the Masked Goddess, son of her church's protector. He comes into this place a son to our queen, and will leave it as a husband and man in his own right."

Somehow, the words sounded more like a sentence than the wish for future happiness they were probably intended to be. He kept walking, while around him, masked figures threw flower petals. Sebastian kept going until he reached the front of the hall, turning in place to face the sea of guests in front of him.

Musicians started to play at one side of the room, a harpist and a lutenist working in concert while a collection of choristers sang together and the high priestess started to speak the welcoming words for a wedding.

"Brothers, sisters, children of the Masked Goddess, we gather at moments like this for the shifting of roles from one to another, shedding our previous selves and becoming someone new…"

Sebastian tried to concentrate on the words, but he still couldn't keep himself from thinking about Sophia. He'd been planning this moment with her before he'd found out about her being one of the indentured. He'd been ready to stand beside her and say the vows that would make them into husband and wife.

He looked around the room again. To his surprise, he couldn't locate Rupert. Had his brother really decided not to show up for Sebastian's wedding? Maybe he'd forgotten, or had just decided that it would be more fun to go off fighting. Probably he would show up for the wedding feast, just in time to drink all of the wine.

"Is there any reason why this union should not take place?" the high priestess asked. Sebastian saw her look over to the spot where his mother sat. "Does the queen give her consent for this union?"

"She does," his mother said, looking happier than Sebastian had thought she might in this moment. She actually looked proud of him as he stood there. Sebastian wished he felt proud of himself. Instead, everything just felt... wrong.

It shouldn't feel wrong. In the time since he'd learned Sophia was still alive, Sebastian had felt hope for the first time since... well, for the first time since he'd seen her apparently dead in the ship's cabin. That hope had filled everything, but with every moment this ceremony progressed, Sebastian could feel more of it dripping away.

He stared at the two masks that had been made for him and Angelica. They were indeed beautiful, made with silver and diamonds so that they seemed to shine with their own inner light. One had delicate, feminine features that somehow managed to capture some of Angelica's beauty, while the other had stronger, more powerful lines. They should have been symbols of the bright future to come for both of them, but instead, Sebastian found himself looking at them as if they were shackles.

Then Angelica arrived.

To say that she looked perfect wasn't enough to do her justice. Even with the plainness of the mask used on the journey to the altar, she was stunning. Her dress was simple white, but Sebastian had never known that there could be so many subtle shades of it, each one clearly used to perfection by a master dressmaker. Four attendants carried her train, while a couple of young children accompanied her, scattering saffron powder that quickly added color to the dress in an effect that Sebastian suspected was deliberate, turning her from something pure but blank to something golden as she advanced.

Her every step felt like a dance, every movement she made as though it had been sculpted for its elegance. Sebastian couldn't look away, and yet, at the same time, his thoughts weren't of the woman who was about to become his bride.

Every movement Angelica made had him thinking of the way Sophia might have moved. Every touch of theatricality had him thinking of the simplicity she preferred. Even the gold of Angelica's carefully coifed hair had Sebastian thinking of the flame red of Sophia's.

"When your bride reaches you," the high priestess said beside Sebastian, "remember that you are to look into one another's eyes while I say the blessing of the goddess, then remove one another's masks so that I can begin the ceremony of marriage."

Sebastian nodded numbly. He knew what he was supposed to do. The problem was that he didn't know what he *wanted* to do. No, that wasn't true. He knew what he wanted. He knew *who* he wanted.

Yet here, now, like this, it really wasn't the moment for thoughts like that. If Sebastian had mentioned them to anyone, he was sure they would simply have dismissed them as last-minute nerves, mourning for what might have been. Either that, or they would have reminded him of his duty in a time when the kingdom was at war. The people needed this.

"And what about what I need?" Sebastian whispered to himself.

"What was that, your highness?" the high priestess asked.

Sebastian shook his head. "Nothing important."

Except that it was important. The thoughts of Sophia filled his head, feeling like a betrayal with each remembered glimpse of her, since it was Angelica walking toward him like a vision from a dream. Nothing was more important right then than the fact that she was still out there somewhere, alive, and safe, and waiting. No, one thing was more important:

The fact that she still loved him.

She'd written that much. She'd told Sebastian to come to her in Ishjemme. She'd told him that he was going to be a father, and that seemed so important that he might have torn the world apart if he needed to.

Sebastian was still thinking about that when Angelica moved to stand in front of him, moving with the kind of grace that made her dress swirl around her.

"It's time," the high priestess said. "Unmask one another in the sight of the Goddess, of your families, and of your friends. See who you really are and declare your love. Declare that you are ready for this marriage."

That was a traditional part of the ceremony. No one could be made to marry until they had seen their intended. The church said that it was that you had to see the truth of someone before you could give yourself to them. Sebastian had heard that it was because, in the past, unscrupulous people had made a habit of substituting themselves for the wedding's intended partners.

Sebastian reached up to remove the mask from Angelica's face and felt Angelica's fingers touch his face as she gently lifted the mask from his features in turn. Even here, like this, Sebastian found himself half-expecting, half-*hoping*, that he would see Sophia's face there beneath the mask. That somehow she would have found a way.

Except that it wasn't up to her now, was it? It was up to him.

"Sebastian," Angelica said. "Are you all right? You look… you look *disappointed*."

She sounded as though she couldn't believe that, and Sebastian could understand it. What kind of man could ever be disappointed with her? The answer to that was simple: a man who was already in love.

"Are you ready to be married?" the high priestess prompted. "Declare your love, so that I may begin."

"I declare my love," Angelica said. "I want to marry this man."

Sebastian knew that was his moment to reply in kind. It would only take a few words, and he would have done his duty. Instead, he stood there, staring.

"Sebastian," Angelica said.

Sebastian knew he'd already hurt her once, and he shouldn't do it again. He shouldn't run from her, not here, not like this. There was only one place he wanted to be, though, and it wasn't marrying Angelica.

"I'm sorry," Sebastian said. "I can't… I can't do this."

He stepped away, starting for the door and pushing past the people before they could realize what was happening. He needed to get out of the castle, out of the city, out of the country. He made it to the door before Angelica's scream of rage sounded behind him.

He needed to get to Ishjemme.

CHAPTER TWENTY SIX

Endi was running out of patience. He sat in one of the reception rooms at the castle, having to feign enjoyment while he, Sophia, and Oli listened to Rika giving a performance on the harp.

It wasn't that Rika's playing was bad. She was a skilled musician, and her voice always put Endi in mind of the gentle pouring of a waterfall. It was just that Endi couldn't enjoy such things when their birthright was being stolen from beneath them.

Why hadn't his assassin acted yet? Had Bjornen lost his skills?

"Wonderful," Sophia said, clapping as Rika finished, her forest cat companion twining around her legs. "I wish I were half as talented."

"And I wish *I* had half *your* talents," Rika said. She always was sweet to people, but that was too much. Why give someone compliments who was already being given more than enough, in the form of your family's home?

"Yes," Endi agreed. "Well played, Rika."

He was just grateful that he was one of the siblings who had learned to close themselves off to those with powers. If he'd been as simple and open as his sister, Sophia would have known about his assassin long ago. Probably she would have set that fighting mad sister of hers, Kate, after him.

Where *was* Bjornen? Surely the man had to see that they couldn't wait forever?

Almost as if in answer to Endi's thoughts, a servant came in, bearing a scrap of paper. Endi thought nothing of it at first; he made a point of keeping track of things in the city.

"Another of your spies, brother?" Rika asked with a laugh. She made it sound as if it were all a game.

"You make me sound grander than I am," Endi said. "The others fight, Oli learns everything, you sing. The least I can do is watch for trouble."

He was expecting no more than that when he opened the note. A scrap of rumor perhaps. A message that some trader had learned about events in the war. Instead, it made him freeze in place.

The younger is away, so now is the time. Get her out of the castle and I will do the rest. B.

Endi hadn't been certain that the big man could write. He pushed that thought aside though, just as he pushed aside the annoyance that Bjornen wanted him to do so much of the work. Already, he had the beginnings of a plan.

"It seems I have to go up to the northern watchtower," Endi said. He looked around. "Some trouble there. Sophia, have you been that far out yet? Would you like to see some more of Ishjemme?"

Let them think that he was playing the same game Jan was. At least that would mean they got to go there undisturbed.

"I'd like that," Sophia said. She turned to the others. "What about you two?"

"I've reading to do," Oli said, reliable as always.

"I'll go," Rika volunteered.

Endi cursed silently. He should have thought of that, but he'd been banking on Rika wanting to practice her harp more. Now, he couldn't think of a reason to leave her behind that wouldn't put Sophia off as well. He forced a smile.

"Then let's go. It sounded quite urgent."

Plus, he wanted to be sure that he got through this before Kate got back. She was far more dangerous than her sister, and he doubted that even Bjornen would be able to take both of them.

They hurried from the castle, and Endi made sure he got them out of there as quickly as he could, before Frig or Ulf or Hans could decide to join them. Rika wouldn't fight off an assassin, but one of the others might try, and Endi didn't want his family hurt. Just the ones who were trying to steal Ishjemme from them.

"This way," Endi said, leading the way through the city, heading for the northern watchtower.

"Slow down a *bit* at least?" Rika called from behind him.

"There's no time," Endi called back. The truth was that he wanted to set a good pace deliberately. He had to judge it well, though. Too fast, and Sophia might give up, although she currently seemed to be keeping up pretty well, her forest cat loping along beside her. Too slow, and he would be walking beside them whenever Bjornen struck, and he would be expected to intervene.

Endi didn't have any of the talents that ran in his family's blood, but he could practically feel the assassin watching them now. He'd done his part. He'd brought Sophia out into the open, and now he just had to wait.

"Rika," he said, drawing his sister away. "Look at this."

When Bjornen leapt, it even took Endi by surprise; the big man moved that quietly. He even moved quietly when he struck, charging forward with an axe in his hand so fast and so quietly that he might have been one of the snow bears he was named for.

It might have worked if Sophia hadn't turned at that moment, obviously warned by some instinct. Endi had thought her soft and easily killed, but to his surprise, she ducked out of the way of the first blow, crying out.

"Help!" she called. "Sienne!"

It was an even greater shock to find that it wasn't the forest cat that leapt to the attack first, but Rika. Bjornen had mistimed his attack with that. He'd left Endi's sister too close, and now she sprang forward. She only had a short eating knife for a weapon, but she stabbed at him, cutting through the big man's tunic and scattering blood.

Bjornen hit her with his axe, and Rika went down with a scream. The shock of *that* was enough to start Endi staggering forward. This wasn't supposed to be how it happened. His sister wasn't supposed to be hurt. This was supposed to be clean, neat.

There was nothing neat about it in the next few seconds, as the forest cat leapt at the big soldier. Teeth and claws tangled with strong arms and the axe, until Endi could barely tell what was happening. There was more blood, while the roars of the man and the cat blended together into one sound.

Endi looked around for Sophia, and she was already moving forward, a knife in her hand. This wasn't a delicate knife like the one Rika had used. This was longer, and obviously designed for killing. Endi hadn't expected that. He'd thought that she was the sister who wasn't interested in fighting. He'd thought that this would be easy.

"Careful," he yelled, although he wasn't sure who he was warning. His eyes found Rika as she lay on the ground, stiller than she should have been, a gash on her head spilling blood onto the earth around her.

Both Bjornen and Sophia seemed to react to his warning, although the soldier moved first. He swung his axe at Sophia again, and again, she barely managed to dodge. The cat, Sienne, leapt into the gap, tearing at Bjornen's legs so that the big man cried out.

Endi drew his sword. It was a long, slender thing that he was sure Hans would have laughed at, especially since he'd seen Endi trying to use it on the training grounds. Even so, Endi advanced.

It would only take one thrust to end this, plunging it deep into the forest cat, or even just driving it through Sophia's throat. If he did that, this would be done with, and the threat Sophia represented to Ishjemme would be gone. He would be able to contact his friend across the water, and he had no doubt that she would be grateful.

Endi started to pad forward, waiting for his moment. He would have to do this quickly and cleanly, before Sophia could use her power to shout for her sister. Put like that, it was obvious that he would have to kill her and hope that Bjornen could hold off the forest cat long enough. He crept around behind Sophia, looking for the best angle from which to strike.

Then he heard the groan, and saw Rika raise her head. It was both brave and incredibly inconvenient, all at once. It was bad enough that his sister was watching a member of Ishjemme's army attacking Sophia. *That* could be put down to the dukedom's many factions. If Rika saw Endi strike Sophia down, there would be no disguising his role in this. There would only be one option, and Endi had no wish to murder his sister. He wouldn't do it.

Perhaps he could delay? No one thought he was a great fighter. Maybe if he left Bjornen alone, the big man might be able to finish this, in spite of the fact that Sophia was holding her own in the fight, with the aid of her cat. Even as Endi watched, she stabbed Bjornen again, but she still had to scramble back as he struck at her once more.

Then Endi heard the one sound he'd been hoping to avoid in this.

"Don't worry, Sophia, I'm coming!"

Jan charged into view like some avenging knight from legend. Endi found himself wondering what his brother was doing there at all. Maybe Oli had told him that Sophia was going for a walk and he had thought to join them. Maybe he was even jealous that Endi was spending time around Sophia. Endi might have laughed at that, except that Jan was a decent fighter, and his presence narrowed the options down considerably.

Endi stepped forward and stabbed Bjornen through the chest. The lunge was clumsy, but the point was sharp, going in through the lung easily enough. Bjornen turned to Endi, looking at him with a mixture of anger and betrayal that Endi would have found faintly amusing if it hadn't all been so serious.

"But why?" he began. "You said that—"

Endi pulled out the sword and cut his throat before he could say more. The big man seemed even more shocked by that than he had by the thrust to the chest. He stared at Endi for a second or two before toppling forward like a falling tree.

In the seconds that followed, things were chaotic. The forest cat was still growling and hissing, while Sophia was trying to calm it.

Endi could have killed her then, if it wouldn't have meant having to kill his siblings too. Jan seemed faintly disappointed, as if Endi had stolen his big moment by finishing off the would-be assassin before he could get there. Rika got to her feet unsteadily, the wound on her head still bleeding.

"We need to get you to a healer," Sophia said. "Maybe my sister could do something."

The best thing they both could have done was die before they got there. As it was, Endi had just wasted his best opportunity to finish this. He would need to find another, or this was only going to get worse. As it was, Milady d'Angelica was not going to be pleased.

Maybe she was having better luck when it came to containing this situation.

CHAPTER TWENTY SEVEN

Emeline stood tied against the iron post, trying not to show any of the terror that she felt. She didn't struggle and throw herself against the ropes, but that was only because she could feel how tight they were, and she knew it wouldn't do any good. Beside her, Cora wasn't so stoic about it. She wrenched at the ropes, as if she might break free; as if she might suddenly have a way through the mass of the villagers who had gathered to watch.

Emeline's approach was simpler: in her mind she shouted with all the strength of her power, throwing it out into the world and hoping that there would be someone there to listen.

Help us, please! They're going to burn us!

"You are evil things," the priestess who had condemned them said as she stood before them. "And you must be purified of that evil, but the Masked Goddess is not without mercy. Repent your sins, beg for forgiveness, and it will be the strangling rope for you rather than the fire."

A part of Emeline wanted to do it. Death by fire was the most horrific way to lose a life she could think of. Just the thought of it made her want to scream and beg. She could see the faces in the crowd though. Parents had brought their children to watch the "witches" burn. Villagers had gathered in numbers Emeline could barely count.

"You want that, don't you?" Emeline said. "You want me to tell you that what you're doing is right. You want me to tell everyone watching that I'm an evil thing. Well, I'm not. I'm just a person like all of you, and you're about to…" Her voice caught. "You're about to burn me to death."

The priestess nodded. "So be it."

Please, if you can hear, they're going to burn us!

Emeline threw the words out again as the villagers around them started to stack wood around her feet. Kindling at the edges, bigger pieces toward the center, moving with a surety that said they'd done this before. There was something ritualistic about it, the same reverence there that might have been present for a marriage, or a funeral.

"Do you know what you're doing?" Cora called out to the people there. "You're standing by and watching while they murder us!"

Emeline admired her bravery, but her own focus was on her power. She knew the townsfolk weren't going to stop, weren't going to change their minds about those with talents. All she could do was call out in ways that went beyond silence, hoping that Stonehome was truly as close as people thought.

And that they cared.

What if they didn't? What if they heard and they were too afraid to come, or too callous? What if they saw no need to help a stranger? Even as Emeline watched, one of the villagers stepped forward with a burning taper, touching it to the edge of the kindling the others had stacked there.

"Please don't," Emeline found herself saying. She could feel the tears stinging her eyes now, and though she wanted to pretend that it was the smoke rising up from the not quite dry wood, she knew that wasn't the truth.

"It will be all right," Cora called over to her. "It will be all right, Emeline."

It sounded as though she was trying to convince herself as much as Emeline. Emeline didn't need her powers to feel the fear there. She could hear it in every syllable as the flames started to catch.

The crowd was jeering now, the pretense of reverence or seriousness long gone. They were enjoying this, reveling in Emeline's and Cora's terror as the first flickers of orange caught on the wood, and grew, building around the edges.

"Praise the Masked Goddess!" the priestess called out. "Who gives us the power to fight against the tainted and the impure! Who gave these into our hands!"

Smoke was rising faster now from the pyre, growing in billowing clouds that made Emeline cough and want to retch as it invaded her lungs. Would the smoke be enough to kill her? Emeline had heard of it happening, when houses had burned back in the city, and once when a butcher had been trapped in his own smokehouse. Smoke took away the space that air needed, it took away the senses...

Maybe it would even be better to die like that. Better a quick fall into unconsciousness than the slow agony of the fire. Even so, Emeline fought to breathe, fought to keep crying out with her powers, fought for any chance at life.

"Help us!" she called out, not even bothering with silence now. "Please!"

She could feel heat building behind her, the iron post heating like a lump of metal in a blacksmith's forge. The heat started as simple warmth, then built into something uncomfortable, and continued to grow.

Beside Emeline, she heard Cora start to whimper with the pain, then cry with it. She cried out herself, the heat too great to do anything else, the ropes leaving no way to get away. She strained to their fullest extent, and still the heat was too much. Worse, the flames were getting closer.

Then she saw the figures rushing into the square, and she knew her mental screams for help hadn't been in vain.

They were as brightly colored as any circus or group of players, unrestricted by the sumptuary laws of the rest of the kingdom. They rushed and they bounded, leapt and ran, not so much an army as a charging group of individuals, no two clothed, or armed, the same way. Only their battle cry was unified, ringing out in the mind in a way that had nothing to do with mouths or air.

For Stonehome!

The townsfolk turned as the newcomers ran in, and Emeline heard their screams even above her own. Some screamed in terror, some in anger, more in pain as swords sliced into them, pistols fired. In a matter of seconds, the heart of Strand was in chaos, with people fighting to get clear, or trying to fight the newcomers.

The ones who did that died.

Some of those who charged into the square were faster or stronger than their frames might have suggested. Some seemed to be moving out of the way of blows with the kind of certainty that came from knowing what their opponent would try next. A couple seemed to be able to make their opponents turn to run, or freeze in place with confusion. They scythed into the waiting townsfolk, cutting through them as they tried to fight back.

Cora might have felt more pity for them if she hadn't been burning to death at their hands.

The pain of the iron post had built into agony now, and she screamed until she was hoarse with screaming, the acrid smoke that rose from the wood filling her mouth with every breath. She couldn't see half of what was happening now, could barely manage to keep her eyes from closing in what Emeline knew would be the last time she ever did it. She couldn't hear Cora anymore.

Around her, the battle continued, but Emeline was starting to suspect that their rescuers wouldn't reach them in time. She coughed and couldn't take the next breath because of the smoke, couldn't even get enough air to scream.

Have faith, sister, we're coming for you.

Albeit slower than we intended.

The voices sounded in her mind, distinct in the subtle ways that only thoughts could be. The first was a woman's, sharp-edged, but with a hint of humor to it. The second was a man's with a sense of reassurance that cut through even the pain.

Emeline couldn't hold on any longer, though; she didn't have the strength. She could feel herself slipping down toward unconsciousness, the darkness rising up to claim her...

Then there were hands pulling her away from the pyre, fingers pulling the ropes from her. She felt her weight being taken, tried to walk, and staggered. Someone laid her down on ground that seemed almost icy cold after the agonizing heat of the fire.

"Tabor, come here, we need a healer!" a woman's voice called.

"I have the other," a man said.

Emeline recognized them as the ones who had spoken in her mind. She felt someone pulling the back of her dress away, and she screamed with the pain of it, because it felt as though they were taking half her skin with it.

"Cora," she managed. "Help Cora."

"Cora is the one tied beside you?" the woman's voice asked. "Don't worry, your normal pet is safe."

"Asha, this isn't the time," the man's voice said. "Tabor, quickly now."

Emeline felt hands touching her back, and she screamed at the touch, but she felt the power there. She screamed as it flowed through her, but she could feel her skin knitting beneath it, the soot and smoke in her lungs rising in the form of bile. Emeline rose to her knees, throwing up the vileness of it, managing to find the strength to look around her.

The square was emptier now than it had been. The townsfolk were either dead or had fled into their homes. Two of the three priestesses lay dead on the ground, while the third stood held between two of the Stonehomers. Behind Emeline, the pyres were no more than embers.

Cora was nearby, looking as weak as Emeline felt, but she was at least alive. An exhausted-looking man Emeline took to be the healer was just moving away from her. A man and a woman stood closer. The man was dark-skinned and tall, bearded but bald, broad-shouldered beneath a long coat and dark tunic. He carried a sword that looked more like a butcher's cleaver than a fencing weapon, along with a blunderbuss that he held one-handed.

The woman wore britches like a man, along with a long coat and broad-brimmed hat complete with a peacock feather in the band. She had pistols crossed in her belt, and a slender sword that seemed designed for dancing around defenses.

"Good," she said, "you're back to us. Tell me, would you like to kill the bitch who hunted you?"

Emeline shook her head. She didn't want to kill anyone now, not even the priestess. She just wanted time and space to recover. She just wanted—

Fast as a snake, the woman drew one of the pistols and fired, shooting the priestess while barely looking. She waited for the powder smoke to clear before she put it back in her belt.

"Fair enough," she said, as the priestess collapsed. "But I find that if a thing needs doing, there's no point being squeamish. I'm Asha. This is Vincente. We heard you calling for help."

"Thank you," Emeline said. She managed to push herself to her feet. "I'm Emeline. This is Cora. Thank you all so much."

"Don't worry about it," Vincente said. "You're one of us, and we help our own."

"We help each other," Asha said. She looked around the wreckage of the town. "We should leave. A few townsfolk are one thing, but someone will send for a regiment eventually."

"They'll wait awhile with the war," Vincente said. "Still, I'd rather be home."

There were so many people there. So many people like Emeline. It was hard to believe that she'd finally found the people of Stonehome.

"It's time for us to go," Asha said, taking her arm. "You're one of us now. Welcome to the family."

CHAPTER TWENTY EIGHT

Sebastian hurried through the palace, making for his rooms at top speed, determined to keep ahead of whoever his mother would send after him. He suspected that she would send servants first, or come herself, and that would at least buy him a little time before he found himself faced with guards determined to keep him there.

Even so, he didn't dawdle. There was no time to change clothes, only to grab a few more and throw them in a bag. No time to sort through his belongings for what he most wanted, only time to grab a sword, a pistol, coin, and a thick cloak. Even that seemed to take too much time. How long would it be before his mother ordered the doors barred?

How long would it be before Sebastian had to fight his way to Sophia?

That was what it would come to, if they tried to stop him. He would fight his way through, because he wasn't going to let anything keep him from Sophia again. She was alive, and she wanted him with her, so Sebastian was going to make it to her side, whatever it took. If he had to fight his way through an entire regiment of the royal army, he would.

It was better to be out of the palace before it came to that, though.

Sebastian hurried through the halls, making it to the main entrance while around him servants stared at him, obviously trying to work out if they should try to stop him. Behind him, Sebastian heard shouts, and he looked back to see guards rushing forward from the building, moving too slowly to ever hope to stop him. Sebastian sprinted forward, down toward the city.

A wave of cheering hit him as he did it, coming from all sides, surrounding him and almost overwhelming him. The shock of it was like the slap of the real sea, and it took Sebastian a moment to remember that there were people out there who had been waiting hours for him to emerge with his bride on his arm, ready to process in a display of royal pageantry. The royal carriage sat waiting for them, an elegantly carved thing that looked more like a table ornament than a conveyance. Sebastian ran for it, leaping into it while the carriage driver looked at him in shock.

"Drive!" Sebastian yelled. "Get me to the docks as fast as you can, or my mother will want to know why!"

That choice of threat would probably protect the man a little from any repercussions. After all, the Dowager expected people to follow her orders. Certainly, the carriage driver didn't question them now. He whipped his team of horses forward, and the great carriage rumbled into motion.

Around it, people continued to cheer, perhaps because they couldn't see that it was just Sebastian in the carriage. Maybe that was what the monarchy was: a big colorful shell for people to cheer, and where it didn't really matter who sat within.

Or perhaps not, because now it seemed that there were some boos mixed in with the cheers, the rumors about what was happening traveling faster than the carriage could. Sebastian could feel people pressing up against the carriage now, wanting to get closer and see what was happening. Looking back, he thought he could see the shapes of horsemen, pushing forward, using their riding crops to force back the crowd. He made a decision.

He kicked open the door and ran down into the crowd, the move shocking enough that he was able to get through the first press of people before they realized what was happening. Sebastian kept running, dodging between them, losing himself amongst the spectators even as he continued to head for the docks.

He would say this for Ashton: its twists and turns were almost designed for losing pursuers, the erratically built houses providing a host of tangled alleys and narrow runs. Sebastian made his way along one, came out the other side, and kept going toward the docks.

"Keep going," he told himself. "Sophia is waiting."

It was all he needed to provide his limbs with fresh strength. He dared to imagine what it would be like, traveling across to her, a ship carrying him north and then east, bypassing whatever fleet the New Army had and then swinging around to make it to Ishjemme. He dared to imagine Sophia standing on the shore waiting for him, looking out over the sea with hope still on her face in spite of all the time they'd been apart.

The docks were ahead now. Sebastian looked out at the forest of masts and realized that he had no clue which, if any, of them were heading in the direction he wanted. All he could do was run down to the dockside, shouting up to them in the hope that someone would hear.

"I am Prince Sebastian," he called out. "I need to get to Ishjemme urgently, and I will pay any man who can get me there."

He called it out again and again, hoping he didn't sound like some madman who had stumbled onto the docks, knowing that the very act of shouting it to the world made it more likely that his mother's men would find him before he got the ship he wanted. Most of the sailors looked down at him as if convinced that he was joking, or drunk, or both. A few more shrugged or shook their heads, obviously not intending to go in anything like the right direction. The business of the war meant that most of them were too busy loading cannon or preparing berths for troops.

"Try towards that end," a man called down, pointing. "I think there were some Ishjemme merchants that way."

"Thank you," Sebastian called up. "You don't know the good you've done with that."

Sebastian ran along the length of the docks, dodging around the crab nets and the cargo crates, avoiding the people who were busy loading their vessels as he tried to seek out the ship that might finally take him to Sophia.

He felt free in that moment. Freer than he'd felt in a long time. He wasn't the dutiful son anymore, or the husband about to be pushed into a marriage that would be good for the nation. He wasn't the soldier who had taken a commission because his mother had decided he needed to earn respect. He wasn't even the son who had been told that he stood to inherit the throne, along with all its problems.

He was just a man hurrying toward the woman who loved him in that moment. He was finally the man he should have been back when he first met Sophia, concerned about nothing but her. She was everything: his love, his hope, the woman who would be the mother of his child. He would be with her, and all the rest of it would fall away like mist.

That sense of freedom lasted right up to the moment he saw Rupert lounging on the edge of the docks, seated on a mooring post shucking an oyster with a knife while a dozen or more men stood around him.

"Ah, brother, there you are," he said.

"What are you doing here, Rupert?" Sebastian demanded. "Come to drag me back the way mother wants again?"

"Well, I considered that," Rupert said. He downed his oyster in one swallow, then casually tossed the shell out into the harbor. "But look at the thanks it earned me. Mother doting on you rather than me, wanting to go with your plan, wanting *you* to succeed. No, I don't think we'll be doing this Mother's way."

Sebastian approached cautiously. "So what then? You'll let me go? I swear to you, Rupert, if you let me cross the sea to Sophia then—"

"Oh, is *that* what this is?" Rupert said. "Your whore is alive? I was wondering what could make you run out like this. Sadly, though, it doesn't work like that. Do you think I'd trust you not to come back, not to try to claim what's mine?"

Sebastian knew that his brother would never see the truth. Rupert couldn't understand that not everyone in the world thought like him. Right then, Sebastian didn't care. He would go through Rupert if he had to.

"No," Rupert said, "there are already plans in place, and they do not include you wandering around as you will." He turned to his men. "Take him."

Sebastian drew his sword, thrusting at the first of the men to come at him. The man barely danced back in time. His pistol barked, and another man fell, wounded in the leg. When it came to getting to Sophia, there was nothing he wouldn't do, no fight he wouldn't take on.

The other men came in, though, and they didn't do it in ones and twos. They rushed for him in a group, and although Sebastian felt his blade pierce one of their flanks, the others were on him as he did it. If they'd been trying to kill him, he would have been cut to pieces in seconds.

Instead, they came at him with fists and clubs, battering Sebastian to the floor and disarming him, holding him firmly as Rupert stepped back into view.

"This was an amusing diversion," his brother said, with a cruel laugh. "But I'm afraid that I don't have enough time to waste more on you now. Don't worry, though, there will be plenty of time for you… later."

He gestured, and Sebastian felt a club crash down on his skull.

He didn't know how many times he slid in and out of consciousness in the minutes that followed. Sensations and sights came to him in short bursts, punctuated by darkness. He had the sense of being carried, and shoved roughly into a cart. He felt the bouncing of cobbles beneath it, and heard the rumble of the wheels. Somewhere beyond, there was the creak of a gate, and then rough hands were dragging him out again, down into a space where the lamplight seemed too bright, hurting Sebastian's eyes.

There was steel at his wrists now, fastened into place with crude locks and rough chains. Hands shoved him forward, and Sebastian staggered, barely able to keep his footing as they shoved him toward a space that was little more than a tiny, stone-walled cell.

"They call this an oubliette," a man said, close to Sebastian's ear. "You'd better pray that your brother forgets you. You wouldn't like the things that happen to the ones he remembers."

They shoved him inside, and Sebastian barely even had the room to collapse. He wanted his last thoughts to be of Sophia, but somehow Rupert managed to invade even that, the memory of his laughter cutting through it, his remembered words promising cruelty to come.

"I'll make time for you later."

Sebastian didn't want to think about what that might mean, not if his brother was already willing to do this. It begged another question, too: what was Rupert doing that meant he had no time?

What was his brother up to?

CHAPTER TWENTY NINE

The Master of Crows didn't betray any emotion as he watched his forces being crushed, in spite of the scale of the reversal. He sat in a camp chair, letting his attention flow through his creatures, while around him, his captains babbled with reports, telling him about the fall of this village or that company. He let it wash over him.

"Dathersford is in ashes, my lord."

"The second company is not reporting back."

"Our eastern cohorts are reporting heavy losses to the fires and the free companies."

They told him nothing that he could not see for himself. The crows flying over the battlefields told him the scale of the enemy's assault, showed him the fires that were sweeping through the peninsula even now.

"Their commander is a ruthless man," he said. "Half of the peninsula is a blackened thing. There will be no crops from it now."

"He wins victories now, but his people will starve in the long run," one of his captains, Olin, said.

The Master of Crows regarded the other man coolly. "The point is that he is winning a victory now. Being able to smirk at his poor statesmanship from our graves is no consolation for being in them."

He had to admit that he had not expected this tactic from his foes. Everything he had learned said that the Dowager and her commanders were conservative in their approach, determined to protect what was theirs rather than just deny it to another. The mind that had come up with *this* plan was more like a knife, sharp-edged and willing to cut through, regardless of the damage.

It wasn't just the fires, although they had claimed many of his men already. The desperation of the free companies was another part of it as they found themselves driven forward by the royal regiments. Even the smallfolk had risen up again, perhaps sensing that they were doomed no matter what they tried.

"Do you have a plan, my lord?" Olin asked. The Master of Crows had the feeling that he had found himself elected by the others to ask the question.

It was a valid one. In a wider space, the Master of Crows might have found a way to prevail anyway. He might have slipped away from his foes and come back at them from a new angle. Caught in this peninsula, there was nothing but the tightening net of flames and steel.

"My plan is a simple one," the Master of Crows said. "Sound the withdrawal."

"The withdrawal?" Olin asked. "But my lord—"

The Master of Crows drew a pistol and shot him in one smooth movement. It wasn't just that he couldn't be seen to be questioned now. He couldn't allow the other man to become a focal point for his captains. That was the way that rebellion lay.

If it helped to assuage some of his annoyance at seeing his troops turned back, that was entirely coincidental.

"We will pull back," the Master of Crows said, in clear tones to prevent any misunderstanding. "We have spent enough time on this island for now, and I have no doubt that problems will be fermenting back on the continent. We will return in due course, but for now, this invasion is done."

None of them argued. None of them dared to when the corpse of their colleague was already attracting its share of ravens. They probably thought of the retreat as an admission of weakness, but the Master of Crows knew better.

He stood, setting off for his flagship while his men hurried to relay his orders. He sent out the command to pull back through his creatures, not caring which units it left exposed.

"Let them die," he muttered. "Let them all die."

That was the part that lesser beings would never understand. They saw their petty wars in terms of winning and losing, conqueror and conquered. There was a point, though, when all of that gave way to a simpler truth: it didn't matter which side was dying, so long as the crows were fed with the energy of the fallen.

Even losing, even pulling back, the Master of Crows could feel that energy flowing into him. Every man who fell to the free companies, every villager caught between the steel of both sides, fed that power. The New Army might not have gained land here, but the Master of Crows' power felt like an ocean he would be able to dip into whenever he needed it.

He stepped lightly onto the deck of his flagship. "Prepare to return home."

They sprang to obey. The Master of Crows looked out at the forces hurrying back to their ships, running to make it to the shore in time to escape, and he laughed, long and loud, at the ruthlessness that had forced them to it.

In the distance, he saw royal standards closing in with the sure steadiness of men who knew that the battle was already won. The Master of Crows stood, drawing one of his blades and essaying a duelist's salute.

Whoever was up there, it seemed that the Master of Crows had finally found a foe sufficiently ruthless to be amusing. Between the two of them, his birds would feast very well in the days to come.

***

Prince Rupert watched the flames from well behind the front lines of the conflict. Only a fool threw himself forward into the teeth of the battle. Besides, between the wounded and the execution of traitors who had dared to surrender to the enemy, the screams here were more than enough to make him smile.

"Your highness," General Sir Launceston Graves said, "it appears… it appears that the enemy is starting to pull back."

"Starting to, General Graves?" Rupert countered. "We've been pushing them back since this started."

The general and the other noble commanders had been squeamish about the plan at first. They'd executed it with grim faces, and executed fleeing soldiers with grimmer ones. They'd acted as if this were all some madman's errand or unpleasant necessity, rather than the obvious thing to do.

"As you say, your highness," the man said. "It seems that your move was… most inspired."

If he was grudging about it, others were more effusive in their praise. One group of the men cheered as Rupert passed them; then another. The truth was that common men didn't interest Rupert, but he understood enough about their uses to wave and smile.

He assessed the land around him. It was blackened and lifeless now, the fire having cleansed it. The shells of buildings stood empty and skeletal, their inhabitants having either fled or put to the sword. Rupert didn't really care which.

He took a horse and rode toward the front, assessing the way things had gone. This was his favorite phase of any battle, when there was no chance of the enemy coming to kill him, only victims to choose.

"There is a cluster of the enemy ahead," Sir Quentin Mires said, arriving on horseback with the air of a man eager not to miss any of the glory. "They are cut off from their ships."

148

"Then let us see what can be done with them," Rupert said. He spurred his horse on, riding forward securely now that he was sure the bulk of the enemy forces were retreating.

There were indeed enemies ahead, their ochre uniforms partly fire-blackened, partly mud-stained. Rupert could see them dug into hollows and wedged behind even the smallest rises in the ground. He tried not to think about how easy it would be for any one of them to send a musket ball his way.

Instead, he thought about how small they looked, and how frightened. Rupert quite enjoyed that thought.

"Shall we send the men forward to wipe them out?" Sir Quentin asked.

It was the obvious thing to do, and if he'd been alone, Rupert would probably have ordered it without hesitation. As it was, he could see the other man watching him, obviously judging him, trying to work out what he would be like in victory. That was the problem with politicians: nothing with them was ever simple, not even their support.

"I think the moment has come to be magnanimous," Rupert said. Sir Quentin almost managed to hide the look of shock that crossed his face. He'd obviously been expecting a slaughter. Rupert made a point, though, of not being the man others expected him to be. If they couldn't predict him, they would always be wary of him.

Besides, this was the kind of moment in which legends were built. Rupert heeled his horse forward.

"Your highness," General Graves called out, barely keeping up with him. "Do you think that is entirely wise?"

"You are both welcome to stay behind," Rupert called out. In fact, he hoped that they would. This would make for a far better image in the minds of those around him if he was alone.

"You there!" he called out. "Men of the New Army! I am Prince Rupert of the House of Flamberg."

He readied himself to huddle down low on his horse's neck, so that the beast would take any musket balls fired his way. If they were going to attack—Rupert didn't think they would, though. He knew when men were broken.

"Your friends are gone, your forces broken. Even as I speak, the Master of Crows retreats. He has abandoned you."

Rupert rode before them now. It made for a more impressive sight, and if one of them did decide to shoot at him, it at least meant that they were likely to miss.

"You have to decide if you want that to mean your deaths, or a chance at life," he called out. "You have seen the kind of foes we can be, but I am also a prince, and a man of my word! So I say this: lay down your arms, and you will not be harmed."

It probably helped that the men there didn't actually know him. If they had, they would have sneered at the very thought of it. They saw what everyone saw though: the golden prince; the man worthy of their awe. One by one, they stood, dropping muskets and pikes, swords and axes. Rupert looked them over, then rode back to Sir Quentin.

"Have the men take them as our prisoners," he said. "Tell them that, from now, the policy of slaughter is to be amended to one of capture." He raised his voice so that the common soldiers might hear him. "I'm sure the Master of Crows will have left a lot behind in his eagerness to run. Gold, weapons, women. What do you say we claim some of it for ourselves?"

That got an answering roar from some of the nearby men. Rupert stood there basking in the adulation for a few seconds, then rode over to General Graves.

"A bold move, your highness," the general said. "I'm sure people will speak of it. Prince Rupert the peacemaker. Prince Rupert the merciful."

Rupert had no doubt they would. It was the main reason he had done it, after all.

"Forget the people, General. I'm more interested in what you think. Do I have your full support now? Both in the Assembly of Nobles and beyond it?"

He saw the general place his hand over his heart in what was probably meant to be some heartfelt gesture. "You do, your highness. You saved the country this day, and you have my support to the death."

"Good," Rupert said with a smile as he watched the prisoners being marched away. At some point, he would have them killed quietly. There was no point in wasting food on enemy mouths. "Now, if you'll excuse me, General, there's a lot I still have to do."

CHAPTER THIRTY

Kate tiptoed through caves that seemed to glow with their own light, not sure if they were reflections of Haxa's home, some strange imaginary place unlocked by the ritual, or something else entirely. Kate only knew that she had to find the piece of her that sealed her pact with Siobhan, if she wanted to be able to undo it.

Haxa had made it sound as if it would be easy to find, yet the corridors branched in every direction, and Kate wasn't sure which of them she was supposed to take. She passed by cave entrances and carefully carved doorways, barred gates and tears that seemed more suited to fabric than to cloth. There were even spaces where the walls gave way to leaves, arches of trees opening onto spaces beyond.

She was walking through one of those spaces now, along a path that seemed to glimmer with silver, while around her the world opened out and shifted, becoming all too familiar. Kate recognized the courtyard of the House of the Unclaimed, although the scale seemed wrong, the space too large. It took her a moment to realize that it stood as she remembered it from the earliest days she'd been there.

There were girls there, in the gray smocks that they were all forced to wear. They moved closer, shouting taunts.

"Look at Kate, thinks she's a boy."

"You're too short, and too ugly for anyone to want you."

"No wonder your parents abandoned you."

Even now, with the distance of memory, the insults hurt. A part of her wanted to rush forward to stop it, but as she took that first step, she saw the faces turning toward her, saw the hunger in the eyes there.

There was a trap in this; Kate was sure of it. If she threw herself into what lay beyond the glittering path, would she be able to step out again? Would the things beyond attack her? Would she find herself trapped in some dark recess of her own memory?

Kate couldn't take that risk. She pressed on, keeping carefully to the path, and around her, the scene shifted.

There were masked nuns there now, standing tall and disapproving, some bleeding from the wounds that Kate had inflicted on them when she'd killed them. They held whips, canes, straps, and more creative instruments of torture. They started toward her, hissing in voices that had nothing to do with humanity.

"You are a thing of evil. You have no place in the world. You deserve punishment for what you are, and for the things that you've done."

They came forward, swinging their weapons, and although it seemed that they couldn't set foot on the path, their implements could still swing across its boundary. Kate made a sound of pain as a cane struck her, and had to resist the urge to fling herself at the nuns. Instead she dodged, moving along the path, forcing herself to keep going even when they called her vile.

The nuns flickered and faded, the House of the Unclaimed going with them. The things that replaced it weren't any better though. Kate recognized the beachfront battlefield at once, complete with shimmering images of both Lord Cranston's men and the invaders. Both sides looked at her with hatred.

"You abandoned us," Lord Cranston said. "You rowed away and left us to fight the war without you."

"You hid what you were," one of his men said. "Until you left us, you lied to us."

Will was there, or an image of him at least. Kate had to remind herself that it wasn't real. "We kissed, and you still left. I could be dead in the war now, and you don't know. You don't *care*."

They came for the path, while the New Army converged from the other side, forming a deadly gauntlet of blades and spears. Kate ran and dodged, throwing herself flat when she heard musket fire and the screams of the dying. Around her, fog rose as it had during that deadly battle, and now she couldn't see the path clearly ahead of her. She had to pick her way along it one faltering step at a time.

"You murdered me."

Gertrude Illiard walked just a step away, not on the path but beside it, as casually as if they'd both been going for a stroll. Her features were purple with the rigor of death, though, her expression fixed into the shock and hurt Kate remembered from the moment when she'd put the pillow over her face.

"I didn't mean to," Kate said.

"You didn't mean to?" Gertrude shot back. "You were the one holding down the pillow. You were the one who pressed down until I stopped struggling."

"I had no choice," Kate said. "Siobhan made me."

"Siobhan made me," Gertrude said, in a parody of Kate's voice. "You sound like a child. If you want to make it better, step

152

off the path. Get what you deserve. You know you deserve it, don't you, Kate?"

Kate didn't reply, pressing onward. The image of Gertrude Illiard was just a reminder of how much she needed to do this, before Siobhan forced her to do anything else.

"Kate, help me!"

Kate spun at the sound of her sister's voice. It came from off the path, and Kate saw her there, bound in place at a post like the one they'd kept at the orphanage.

"Save me, Kate, please!"

Kate almost, almost stepped off the path to help her.

"You aren't the real Sophia," she said with a shake of her head. "You're just an image."

"How can you say that?" Sophia demanded. "I'm your sister. You saved me from the boys at the House of the Unclaimed. We escaped the fire together."

There were figures around her now, pressing in from all sides. There were the masked nuns, and shorter figures Kate recognized as the boys she'd fought off. There were shadowy figures half remembered from the night of the fire, and a version of Prince Sebastian, knife still dripping with her sister's blood.

They converged on the image of Sophia, and Kate couldn't stop herself. Even though she knew this wasn't real, even though she knew that the real Sophia was safe back in Ishjemme, she couldn't stand by and watch this happen. She stepped off the path toward them.

They were on her in an instant, striking at Kate with knives and hands and things that were closer to claws. Kate screamed as wounds opened in her flesh, but she didn't stand still and let them strike at her. She charged them.

In an instant, her sword was in her hand, the runes laid into it glowing red as Kate cut and thrust, rolled and dodged. She thrust the blade through an image of a masked nun, and it flickered into nonexistence. She ducked under a soldier's swing and cut him in half.

Everything was dark around Kate now. There was no sign of Sophia anymore, the image of her having faded in the heat of the battle. Even the path seemed so far distant that it might take an age to reach it. Even so, Kate ran for it.

Claws reached for her, spears thrust at her. Still, Kate ran, fighting as she went. She hacked down foes who wore the faces of friends and enemies alike, their features all twisted into a combination of hunger and hatred that made Kate shiver just to see it. Even the hands of the dead clutched at Kate, trying to slow her down. She ran for the path, plunging through the darkness until her feet found it.

Behind her, the images stopped short as if slamming into an invisible wall.

Kate pressed on, and now she had to stop her ears, because it was Sophia's screams that came from every side. Sophia tortured in a hundred ways, burning alive in the fire that they'd escaped in reality, caught by Prince Rupert, torn apart by the masked nuns.

However, there was no saving what wasn't real, no matter how hard she tried. All Kate could do was press forward, hoping that the silver thread of the path would take her where she needed to go. It felt as though she walked for hours, following the route that the path made her take, until finally, it gave way to grass.

There was no path here. Instead, Kate found herself treading on a carefully kept lawn, a fountain in the middle of it that she knew far too well. Something shined from within the fountain's depths, and somehow Kate knew that it would be what she sought.

She wasn't alone. There was no sign of Siobhan there, but two ghostly figures stood before the fountain, both dressed in fashions that proclaimed them long since dead. Kate thought she recognized them: they'd been among the ghosts Siobhan had sent to kill her, again and again, as she trained.

"This place is not for you," one of the ghosts said, hefting a rapier.

"Turn and leave," the other added, raising a longsword in both hands. "Our mistress has said that none may approach."

"And I *have* to approach," Kate said. "I need to break my deal with her, before she makes me do more things I'll regret."

The one with the rapier shrugged. "If you approach, we will strike. I will not be sent back to the place she keeps those who betray her."

"Nor I," the other man said. He took a defensive posture in front of the fountain.

Kate didn't care. She needed to do this. She stepped forward, blade raised.

Instantly, the rapier wielder attacked, with all the speed and skill that one of those who had drunk from the fountain might possess. He feinted one way, then thrust the other, forcing Kate into a circling parry that barely caught his blade.

"You have skill," he said. "Perhaps even enough to best me in earnest. I cannot allow that."

He gestured and the longsword man came forward.

Kate knew immediately that she was outmatched. She could probably have beaten one of them as they were, maybe both if they'd been alive and susceptible to her powers. Facing two ghosts at once, though, both impervious to pain, both master swordsmen, was too much.

She gave ground, dodging the swings of the longsword, deflecting the rapier. She struck back on instinct, and although her weapon bit into the ghostly flesh thanks to its runes, that flesh healed almost as quickly. Nothing less than a killing blow would work here, and there seemed to be no way to get that.

The best Kate could do was give ground, trying to keep moving so that she never had to engage with more than one of the two at once. Even that didn't give her a way to beat them, though, and she couldn't just dance around forever, not achieving anything while the fountain glowed with power.

In that moment, Kate knew what she had to do.

She feinted right, started left, and then leapt forward as the others moved to intercept her. She ran past them, ignoring their attempt to turn to face her, knowing that she would have moments at most. She could already imagine the two ghosts closing in on her. She leapt up onto the edge of the fountain.

A sphere of energy glowed within, tendrils stretching out from it in waves that disappeared a moment later. It was the size of a closed fist, or a heart. Without hesitating, Kate grabbed it, snatching it up and spinning back toward her sword-wielding foes.

They were almost on her, blades raised for the killing blow. Hoping that she was doing the right thing, Kate raised the sphere of energy, then closed her hand, crushing it.

Around her, the energy exploded.

CHAPTER THIRTY ONE

As soon as she woke the next morning, Sophia went searching for Rika. She had to know that her cousin was all right. Heading for her room, Sophia could see plenty of the others there too, obviously just as concerned with making sure that Rika was all right as Sophia was. The siblings crowded round, while Lars stood trying to mediate the effects of all of them in one place.

He looked over as Sophia approached.

"You, at least, should still be in bed. You need to recover as much as Rika does after an attack like that." He looked around at the others. "I still don't know how a thing like that could happen."

"We were tricked," Sophia said. "None of that matters now. Will Rika be all right?"

"She will recover," her uncle said. "The physikers say that the scar will be very faint."

Sophia winced at the thought that there would be any scar cutting across her cousin's features. If she hadn't been there, there wouldn't have been.

"Maybe Kate can help, the way she helped me," Sophia said. She looked around. "I'm surprised that she isn't here."

Her uncle shook his head. "We haven't seen her this morning, but I will send men to look for her. I am confident that she will be safe."

Sophia hoped so. She knew that Kate could protect herself, but even so, when there were assassins around, it was worrying that she was missing. What was she doing, leaving the castle alone like that?

"For now," her uncle said, "there is news. A ship is approaching; one I think you might be interested in."

Instantly, Sophia's heart leapt with thoughts of Sebastian. Had he gotten her message? Had he finally come for her? Just as soon as that thought came, guilt followed on its heels. She'd sent a message telling anyone who read it where she was. Soon after, an assassin had tried to kill her, hurting her cousin in the process. Was it her fault that Rika had been wounded? Was it her need for Sebastian that had brought danger to them?

No, she realized, with a falling heart. It couldn't be Sebastian. It was too soon, when she'd only just sent the message. Where was the ship from then?

She had her answer soon enough as her uncle smiled. "The vessel is from the Silk Lands."

It took Sophia a moment to realize what he meant. The Silk Lands were where her parents had fled to, the last place that her uncle had heard of them. They'd sent out messages, more in hope than in any expectation that they might be received, yet now there was a ship approaching. Sophia wasn't sure quite how far the Silk Lands were, but she suspected that the ship must have set off almost as soon as she arrived in Ishjemme for it to be here now.

"My parents," she said.

Her uncle spread his hands. "I do not know for sure. There have been no messages, but we get few ships from there. For one to come now… it would be too much of a coincidence. Do you want to go down to meet it?"

Sophia nodded, unable to contain the excitement she felt at the potential the news held. She wanted to run down to the docks and stand there waving until the ship came in to the docks.

"Yes, I want to meet it," she said.

In the end, it was a more sedate walk down to the docks, accompanied by Sienne, who was moving a little stiffly this morning after the fight last night. Sophia moved slowly for the forest cat. After she had saved Sophia's life, the least that Sophia owed her was holding back enough that she didn't make her wounds worse.

Jan came too, officially because there needed to be one of the Skyddars there to meet such far-off visitors, unofficially because after the events of the night before, no one wanted to take chances. He looked over to check on Sophia so often that she found herself blushing with the attentiveness of it all, or maybe not just with that.

She walked down with him through the city, to the space where the ocean spread out before them along the broad bank of the fjord that led out to sea, merchant ships and fishing vessels crowded into the space.

The incoming ship stood out, with its silk sails and its elegant lines. It was swanlike as it moved through the water, slender and serene, even as banks of oars on either side helped to guide it closer. Its woodwork was painted in bright reds and oranges, so that it looked like a flash of sunlight working its way closer to Ishjemme. Small boats moved near to it, obviously there to guide it in closer to shore, but it was clear that someone aboard already knew the best route past the rocks.

Sophia moved to the edge of the docks, waiting as the ship drew closer. Sophia had been to the docks enough times to know

157

that normally, ships were noisy places, the constant yelling of instructions and information necessary to coordinate the actions of all those aboard. This one, though, approached in near silence. It moved up close to the docks, barely brushing them as men threw down slender ropes that nevertheless seemed as strong as steel.

"Are you all right?" Jan asked.

"I just hope that we're not waiting here for a ship full of merchants," Sophia said, trying to make a joke of it, but the truth was that she was worried. What if her parents weren't aboard this ship? What if she *was* just standing there, ready for disappointment when the ship unloaded with no sign of them? What if they'd sent out their messages, and all it had done was remind some Silk Lands noble that Ishjemme existed?

Sophia's hand found Sienne's fur, ruffling it as she waited. The forest cat pressed against her, and Sophia was grateful for her presence. It was a reminder of just how far she'd come, and that she wasn't alone. Even if her parents weren't on this ship, she had a whole family around her in the form of her sister, uncle, and cousins. She wasn't the girl she had been, waiting in an orphanage with no one to rely on but Kate.

Even so, Sophia held her breath as sailors set a gangplank in place between the ship and the shore.

"Let them be there," she whispered, then bit her lip, not wanting anyone to hear.

A figure stepped onto the gangplank, a slender man, swathed in a cloak whose inner lining shone with a dozen colors. He moved with the grace of a swordsman, and Sophia could see a light blade on his hip along with a curved knife. His clothes were strange, wrapping silks, hinting at foreign lands.

When he pulled back the hood of his cloak, though, his features were familiar ones, and the shock of red hair was a giveaway, even if it was strangely cut, shaved on one side and braided with gold strands on the other. He was younger than Sophia might have thought he was, though, certainly not old enough to be her father, probably younger than her.

Who was he then? Sophia could feel a sense of connection just looking at him, could feel the sense of power at the edges of her mind that said he was family. He looked back at her, and when he smiled, a broad and familiar smile, it took away all of the seriousness from his features.

He didn't speak. He didn't have to.

She heard his words as clearly in her mind as if he had just spoken them. That stunned her. There was no one else in the world who could send thoughts to her like that, so clearly, so naturally.

And what stunned her even more were the words he sent.

Hello, sister

.

A JEWEL FOR ROYALS
(A Throne for Sisters—Book Five)

"Morgan Rice's imagination is limitless. In another series that promises to be as entertaining as the previous ones, A THRONE OF SISTERS presents us with the tale of two sisters (Sophia and Kate), orphans, fighting to survive in a cruel and demanding world of an orphanage. An instant success. I can hardly wait to put my hands on the second and third books!"
--Books and Movie Reviews (Roberto Mattos)

From #1 Bestseller Morgan Rice comes an unforgettable new fantasy series.

In A JEWEL FOR ROYALS (A Throne for Sisters—Book Five), Sophia, 17, gets word that Sebastian, her love, is imprisoned and set to be executed. Will she risk it all for love?

Her sister Kate, 15, struggles to escape the witch's power—but it may be too strong. Kate may be forced to pay the price for the deal she made—and to live a life she doesn't want to.

The Queen is furious at Lady D'Angelica for failing to woo her son, Sebastian. She is prepared to sentence her to the Lead Mask. But Lady D'Angelica has her own plans, and she won't go down so easily.

Cora and Emeline finally reach Stonehome—and what they find there shocks them.

Most shocking of all, though, is Sophia and Kate's brother, a man who will change their destinies forever. What secrets does he hold about their long-lost parents?

A JEWEL FOR ROYALS (A Throne for Sisters—Book Five) is the fourth book in a dazzling new fantasy series rife with love, heartbreak, tragedy, action, adventure, magic, swords, sorcery, dragons, fate and heart-pounding suspense. A page turner, it is filled with characters that will make you fall in love, and a world you will never forget.

Book #6 in the series will be released soon.

"[A Throne for Sisters is a] powerful opener to a series [that] will produce a combination of feisty protagonists and challenging circumstances to thoroughly involve not just young adults, but adult fantasy fans who seek epic stories fueled by powerful friendships and adversaries."

--Midwest Book Review (Diane Donovan)

About Morgan Rice

Morgan Rice is the #1 bestselling and USA Today bestselling author of the epic fantasy series THE SORCERER'S RING, comprising seventeen books; of the #1 bestselling series THE VAMPIRE JOURNALS, comprising twelve books; of the #1 bestselling series THE SURVIVAL TRILOGY, a post-apocalyptic thriller comprising three books; of the epic fantasy series KINGS AND SORCERERS, comprising six books; of the epic fantasy series OF CROWNS AND GLORY, comprising 8 books; and of the new epic fantasy series A THRONE FOR SISTERS. Morgan's books are available in audio and print editions, and translations are available in over 25 languages.

Morgan loves to hear from you, so please feel free to visit www.morganricebooks.com to join the email list, receive a free book, receive free giveaways, download the free app, get the latest exclusive news, connect on Facebook and Twitter, and stay in touch!